SECRET LIVES AND PRIVATE EYES

SECRET LIVES AND PRIVATE EYES

HEATHER WEIDNER

TORONTO • NEW YORK • LONDON
AMSTERDAM • PARIS • SYDNEY • HAMBURG
STOCKHOLM • ATHENS • TOKYO • MILAN
MADRID • WARSAW • BUDAPEST • AUCKLAND

WORLDWIDE™

Recycling programs
for this product may
not exist in your area.

ISBN-13: 978-1-335-90106-4

Secret Lives and Private Eyes

First published in 2016 by Koehler Books. Reprinted in 2021 by Sandpiper Productions with revised text.
This edition published in 2023.

For questions and comments about the quality of this book, please contact us at CustomerService@Harlequin.com.

Harlequin Enterprises ULC
22 Adelaide St. West, 41st Floor
Toronto, Ontario M5H 4E3, Canada
www.ReaderService.com

Printed in U.S.A.

To Stan,
Thanks for all of your love and support.

PROLOGUE

"HEY, DO YOU want another drink?" slurred the man on the barstool next to Delanie Fitzgerald.

Delanie leaned in closer. "No, but I'd like to go somewhere and get to know you better. What do you think about that?" she asked, winking at the fifty-something sitting next to her. She tossed her long red curls to one side and tilted her head toward him. She hoped the black dress showed enough cleavage to do the trick.

He smiled. He looked like he was expecting her to kiss him. When she didn't, he waved to the bartender for the tab.

The man placed two twenties on the bar next to his glass. Delanie slid off the barstool, careful not to cause her micro-dress to creep any higher. Flipping her shiny purse strap over her shoulder, she made her way out through the crowd. Delanie felt his ragged breaths on the back of her neck, huffing and puffing like he'd run three or four laps. He reached out and touched her shoulder, trying to steady himself.

When they arrived at the parking lot, she said, "I'm over there. I'll follow you. Where to?"

"I dunno. I'm not from this part of town."

"We could go to your place," she suggested.

"Uh, no. Too far. It wouldn't be any fun."

"Well, I'm all about fun. Okay, where then?" She shivered and wished she had brought a jacket, but it would have ruined the effect.

"Uh, I dunno," he stammered. "I think they're some places over near the interstate a couple of blocks from here."

"Okay. I want somewhere nice with a Jacuzzi."

"I didn't bring a swimsuit."

"Neither did I," she said.

He leered at Delanie, taking in her long legs and short skirt, while fishing through his pockets for his keys.

"I'm in the beige Corolla down there," he said.

She climbed in her black Mustang and watched him stagger to his car.

Delanie felt a tinge of guilt for letting him drive drunk, but she needed to get him at a motel. She started the engine. He still hadn't made it to his car. After turning on the lights and the radio, she kicked off the four-inch heels that pinched her feet and made her calves burn. She threw them in the backseat and settled in to watch what he would do next.

He finally backed out, and Delanie followed behind him until he pulled into a small motel at the entrance ramp to I-95. The sign under the neon vacancy advertised Jacuzzis and free breakfast.

He parked and walked over to her car. Rolling down the window a crack, she waited. He leaned forward but didn't say anything.

"Why don't you get us a room?" she asked. "I'll pull around back and wait for you to get everything ready."

"Okay." He smiled again and wandered off in the direction of the office. It was twelve thirty-five according to the radio display.

Pulling the tiny video recorder out of the backpack she always kept in the front seat, Delanie made sure she captured him going into the office and talking to the desk clerk. Before he returned, she drove around back and parked midway down the row. She turned her lights off and waited in the seedy parking lot, dotted with mostly working lampposts.

A few minutes later, the Corolla parked at the end of the row. Her date weaved up the outside steps to the second floor. Recording his ascent, she zoomed in on the room number before he opened the door. She wasn't sure what he was waiting for.

When he went inside and turned on the lights, Delanie clicked the camera off and flipped her lights on. Backing out, she pointed her car toward the interstate.

Her conversation with Mrs. Clayton tomorrow wouldn't be pleasant, but it was probably expected. Delanie had enough evidence on the camera and the wire taped to her stomach to make the divorce attorney drool. This one was easy. She didn't have to do anything for the setup but hang out in his favorite bar. He found her there and started chatting her up. Another working Friday night, and Delanie Fitzgerald couldn't remember the last time she had a date she didn't have to secretly tape.

ONE

DELANIE SLID OUT of her car and pulled her sunglasses down from her curls to block the blazing afternoon sun. Grabbing her backpack, coffee, and purse, she bumped the car door with her right hip and clicked the key fob twice, listening to the door locks click.

On her way to the office, she shuffled everything to one side and jammed the key into the mailbox, snatching a handful of bills and junk mail addressed to Falcon Investigations.

The receptionist desk, empty as always, remained from the previous tenant. Her suite included a kitchenette, a conference room, and two offices. Small by most standards, the space worked for Delanie and her partner, Duncan Reynolds. Delanie and Duncan would be turning forty in a few years, but each could easily shave at least five years from their ages because of their youthful looks and adventurous spirits. They had been good friends since college. Delanie had used her share from her father's estate to get her PI license and open the firm about seven years ago after business school didn't lead to anything interesting.

Tossing the mail on her desk, she yelled, "Hey, Duncan! Dunc, you here?"

A muffled "Hey," came from the kitchen area. She

followed his voice to find Duncan's feet sticking out from under the sink.

"What's up?" she asked, stepping over Margaret, Duncan's three-year-old English bulldog whose normal speed was napping. Margaret, who only moved for treats and for Duncan, looked like a brown and white log with legs. She wasn't much security, but she was good company.

"We sprang a leak. And we'll need a raft if we wait for maintenance," Duncan muttered from under the sink.

"You okay?"

"Yep," he replied. "I'm almost done. I think I fixed the problem."

"You know I appreciate you. If the computer stuff doesn't work out, I'll put in a good word for you to take over for the maintenance guys."

"Funny," he replied, standing up and wiping his hands on his jeans. He tested the faucet; the leak had stopped. Duncan, a computer geek, worked with Delanie on her cases when she could afford to pay him. The rest of the time, he paid for his office with website design and computer research, which Delanie believed was a euphemism for his extracurricular hacking activities. But he always found interesting information for her, so she never asked where it came from.

"I finished Mrs. Clayton's case last night. You know, the wayward husband investigation. I gave her a copy of his misadventures, and she gave us a check. Whooo hoooo, paying clients."

"Maybe things are picking up," he said. "We received a voicemail from someone interesting in California."

"Cheating spouse or insurance fraud?" she asked, grabbing a water out of the small fridge.

"Neither. A personal assistant for an author in Hollywood. They need a PI to run down some leads."

"How'd the assistant find us?" asked Delanie.

"Our fantastic website, of course."

"What are you waiting for? Let's see what it's about."

Dropping her purse and gently setting her cup of coffee on her desk, Delanie plopped down in her faux leather chair. Duncan leaned on a stack of papers piled on the edge of her desk. She glanced at the back of his computer, a montage of brightly colored stickers for crazy causes and interesting places. He scooted forward, and she punched the phone number for California and pressed the speaker button while Duncan clicked away on his laptop.

After several digital tones, a raspy voice answered, "Tod Eastman."

"Mr. Eastman, this is Delanie Fitzgerald from Falcon Investigations."

"Oh, hi," he said. "Let me put the top up. I'm in the car. Gimme a minute." After a long pause, he returned with, "Sorry about that. My employer is looking for a private investigator in Virginia to do some research for her."

"What type of research?" Delanie asked. She wondered if he was tooling around in some exotic convertible.

"It's for Tish Taylor. Heard of her?"

"Is she the one who writes all those unofficial Hollywood biographies?" Delanie asked.

"That's the one," Tod said. "Sex and sin sell books. Would you be interested in the assignment?"

"Possibly." She tried not to sound too eager. She was glad that Tod couldn't see them. Duncan's head was nodding so vigorously his ears almost flapped. He flipped his laptop around so Delanie could see Tish Taylor's latest tell-alls on infamous celebrities and politicians.

After a half-hour discussion of logistics, reports, and prices, Tod said, "Okay then. I'm pretty sure you can do this work for us. I'll send you a confidentiality agreement. Send it back signed, and I'll FedEx a package of what we have so far. We can work out any other details when it arrives. Send me your contract and fee schedule."

"Sounds good," said Delanie as she disconnected. Duncan pumped the air with his fist and did his happy dance around Margaret. The bulldog joined in the celebration by opening one eye.

DELANIE SLIPPED OFF her red leather sandals and enjoyed their good fortune, landing a client who wasn't trying to dig up dirt on a cheating spouse. On his way out of her office, Duncan said, "Now, this should be interesting. Tish Taylor's recent books have been on former vice presidential candidate John Edwards, Lindsay Lohan, and Michael Jackson's doctor."

She answered the ringing phone as Duncan and Margaret retreated to his office.

"Falcon Investigations."

Delanie managed to get in "yes" and "no" a few times, and then agreed to meet a prospective client downtown in an hour. *Business just might be picking up.* They hadn't had more than one client at the same time in years. It would be nice not to have to worry about the bills for a while.

A few minutes before her appointment, Delanie paid the Honor Park box at the lot across from Gator's Sports Bar. She wondered if her new client would be as chatty in person as he was on the phone.

Inside the restaurant, she marveled at the flat screens lining the perimeter. All the high-tech gizmos contrasted with the rest of the room, which looked like the other rehabbed Civil War warehouses in Richmond's Shockoe Bottom. She didn't see anyone waving at her, so she let the hostess seat her in a booth where she could see the large glass doors. Delanie ordered iced tea and waited.

Midway into her second glass, a tall man with longish blond hair slid into the seat across from her. His shirt was plum and unbuttoned at the collar. The shiny gray suit made Delanie a bit wary of its owner.

"Hey, there. I hope you haven't been waiting long." She was the only female sitting alone, so she was probably easy to spot. He put a phone with a large screen and a pair of Oakley sunglasses on the table. Delanie took note of the small green tattoo of a stylized teardrop under his right eye. She guessed he was about six-foot-three, and his frame filled almost the entire booth across from her. She wondered uneasily if the teardrop meant that he had killed someone.

Before Delanie could reply, he put out his hand and said, "I'm Charles Wellington Smith, but everyone calls me Chaz. Like I told ya on the phone, I own a club, the Treasure Chest, and I'm in need of a private eye." The waitress appeared, and he didn't miss a beat. "I'll have a Corona with lime and the chicken and riblets meal. What about you?"

"I'm fine with the tea for now. Thanks." When the waitress retreated, she continued. "So, Mr. Smith. Why do you need the services of a private investigator?"

"Chaz, please. I own a gentleman's club that's located one block over on Main Street. I've also bought an old restaurant in the museum district, where I want to open a second club. The hoity-toity neighborhood association wants the property refurbished, but not by me. They're making noise, and now, my permits are on hold. I can't open a gentleman's club without a license to serve alcohol or an occupancy permit. It seems that they don't want me near the Fan district or anywhere near their children."

She knew immediately where he was talking about. If you looked at a map of the streets in that older Richmond neighborhood, they looked like they fanned out instead of running parallel like a traditional grid. Newcomers to the area always got lost in the warren of streets.

"So, is this the first time you've had issues with the city or its licensing bodies?"

"Well, uh, no. We've had disagreements over our liquor licenses a couple of times, but I was assured by my lawyers that this was a done deal, and that I would be welcome in the neighborhood. Now, they've built up this grassroots social media campaign against me. They don't see it as a club. They think it's a sexpool for degenerates. And just about everyone is jumping on the bandwagon. The last time I checked, a band of mommy bloggers had made me public enemy number one. My business doesn't fit with the Victorian flair of the neighborhood. Plus, they don't want my club near their precious museums and art galleries. They think that I'm going to ruin the neighborhood. Hell, I'm putting a thriving business in an abandoned building."

The waitress placed a platter of food in front of him. Delanie asked, "What exactly do you want Falcon Investigations to do?"

"I need you to follow up about the licensing and to do some poking around my neighbors-to-be. The president of the neighborhood association is Ken McDermott, a close friend of the mayor's wife. I think this goes deeper than the neighborhood watch. I think someone's calling in favors. We've had a lot of police presence in and around my club recently, and I've gotten four parking tickets in the last couple of weeks. My clients are starting to complain about being harassed by cops."

"Okay, Mr. Smith, uh Chaz, my partner and I will look into your situation. I need you to send me contact information for your attorneys and any people you think are involved. Falcon Investigations charges an hourly fee, plus expenses. It may take at least three or four days for the research."

"I'm fine with that." He took a bank envelope from an interior pocket and slid it across the table. "Start with this as an expense account. And here's a list of everyone I think might have it in for me." The list was big enough to be stapled.

Delanie pulled out a contract and filled in the advance at the bottom. She pushed it across the table, and Chaz signed without reading it. He handed her a business card for the Treasure Chest, *Richmond's Finest Gentleman's Club.*

"Is there anything else that you can think of that relates to your issues with the new property?"

"Uh, nah," he said, wiping sauce off his round chin. "The increased police presence started after we applied for our permits. I know it's not a coincidence. Someone's out to get me. When can you start?"

"We'll start today. I'll call you in a day or two with what we find about your permits."

"That works. Anything else you need from me?" he asked.

Delanie shook her head and stood. She offered her hand, and he licked the sauce from his before shaking. She tried not to cringe. "Thank you. We'll send you an update in a few days."

"I look forward to it." He picked up his phone and started tapping on the screen.

DELANIE STEPPED OUT into the oppressive Richmond heat. She wasn't sure how people survived before air conditioning.

She crossed the cobblestone street and immediately spotted Chaz's vehicle parked next to the curb. It was a purple Hummer II, wrapped in advertising for the Treasure Chest with gold rims and giant pictures of faceless bikini-clad women on every side. His URL and phone number appeared across the top of each girl's bikini. There wasn't anything subtle about Chaz Smith, including the envelope in her purse with a three-thousand-dollar retainer.

TWO

THE NEXT MORNING, Delanie accelerated out of the gas station parking lot, weaving around cars trying to get to the pumps. Her phone rang, and Duncan's cell number popped up on the radio screen. Putting her orange smoothie in the cup holder, she said, "Hey, Duncan, what's new?"

"Tod Eastman, the guy from California, called. He got the contract and the confidentiality agreement you signed. He said that we'd have the box later today. We'll talk when it arrives. And your new buddy Chaz called twice. He thought of more names to add to his public enemy list. He wants you to meet him for lunch this week."

"Oh, goody," she said as she passed a tractor-trailer on her way toward the city. "He's my new BFF, but we can't fuss too much because he gave me a fat retainer to work on his issues. I'll call him later."

"Your new best friend is a strip club owner?"

"Yep, he's Webster's definition of sleaze, but he gave us three grand."

"That'll make it tolerable for a while. The company you keep; and you wonder why you're still single."

"You're one to talk. You hang out with Margaret on weekends. I'm gonna do some snooping downtown. Take a look at Chaz's list and see what kind of magic you can work. Call me if anything jumps out. He thinks the city, the ABC board, and the police are targeting him."

"They probably are. I didn't find anything specific about governmental agencies targeting him, but I did uncover something interesting about his downtown club. Here's my history factoid for the day. It's near the site where Edgar Allan Poe worked as a writer for the *Southern Literary Messenger*. I'll see ya when you get here," he replied. She clicked the button on the steering wheel to end the call. "Call Ami Lawrence work," she commanded, and the car dialed the number. She wondered what Edgar Allan Poe would think of his little part of Richmond being augmented with Chaz's Treasure Chest.

After a couple of rings, she heard, "*Essence Weekly*, this is Ami."

"Hey, lady. This is Delanie, and I'm hoping you have a minute or two for me."

"Well, actually, we're working on next week's spread, and I'm kinda pushed for time."

"I promise I won't bother you too long. I have a new client by the name of Charles Wellington Smith. It seems he's trying to open a new venture in the Fan area, and he's getting a lot of pushback from the city and the home-owners association. The good people of the neighborhood aren't interested in his kind of redevelopment. Heard any rumblings?"

Ami, a feature editor and reporter for a small community arts and popular culture weekly paper, replied, "Are you referring to Chaz, the T&A king?"

"The man, the myth, and a legend in his own mind."

"Let's see," Ami said. She clicked keys and rustled

around. "He landed a good deal on a rundown property that went bankrupt. It was this really quaint neighborhood restaurant in a decent-sized building that dated to the late eighteen hundreds. The dining room was beautifully decorated, and the locals loved the place. After the restaurant went belly-up, it stood vacant for almost four years. Chaz was banking on pushing through all the permits and opening a second strip club without drawing too much attention. He thinks he's improving the neighborhood. In his mind, a strip club that pays taxes is better than an empty building on Broad Street. He wants to be treated like any other respectable businessman. And he doesn't understand why people don't take him seriously."

"Hmmmm." Delanie could think of a few reasons, but she kept quiet in hope that Ami would continue talking. She merged onto Route 288 South and sped into the acceleration lane. The Mustang handled the curve of the ramp with ease.

"Well, our good friend didn't count on the determination of the neighborhood association. The property isn't in the historic district or the Fan, but it's close. It seems the homeowner prez goes to church with some high-ranking city officials. And annoying Chaz has become their new pet project."

"So, strings were pulled to slow down the permits," Delanie said.

"Sounds like it. Maybe they're trying to stall him long enough so he either runs out of money or gives up in frustration."

"Chaz complained that the police were targeting his clientele at the other location. He feels he's getting a lot of unfair attention lately." Delanie changed lanes to pass a semi with two trailers.

"He complains a lot," Ami continued. "And he seems to draw attention wherever he goes. He likes stunts and drama and seeing his name in the paper too. When he couldn't get his permit to open the club on Broad Street, he hired graffiti artists to decorate the outside. At first, the neighbors were upset hoodlums tagged their neighborhood. Then the HOA went berserk when they found out Chaz paid for it. They're still fuming that no one would be charged with defacing the property. They declared war, and it looks like they're going to fight him at every turn. He tried to spin it as if his restaurant is a showcase for urban art and young, budding artists, but I don't think anyone bought it."

"Sounds like a colorful guy."

"He's got a long history of being just on the line between what's legal and what's not. And he's never close to what's 'decent and proper.' I'll go through our archives and send you a sampling of what we have. He's something else. His notoriety goes back to the early '90s."

"You're the greatest, Ami."

"Remember me if you find anything juicy," the reporter said.

"I always do. You're my one-and-only media star."

"And you're my best unidentified source. Peace, love, and all that," Ami said.

"You too, and thanks again." Delanie clicked off the phone.

DELANIE, BLESSED BY two older brothers, dialed the younger one in hopes of getting the latest gossip on Richmond's club scene. He didn't answer after four rings, so he was probably still sleeping. Robbie, a bouncer at Club Echo downtown, knew the River City's nightlife. She would try him again later to see what he knew about Chaz and the Treasure Chest. Changing her mind about a trip downtown, she turned off the highway and backtracked to the office.

Fifteen minutes later, Delanie was sitting in a chair in her conference room. Dropping a FedEx box on the oval oak table, Duncan said, "We received a package from California. I'm guessing it's from Tod Eastman, our Hollywood guy." He plugged his laptop into the projector as she tore into the box.

She gasped, and Duncan looked up. "You okay? Somebody send you a snake again?"

"No, better. And in my defense, it was a rubber snake from one of the guys who didn't like that I took pictures of him and the girlfriend for his wife. This is a box full of Johnny Velvet stuff."

"The one with The Vibes? From the '80s?"

"Yep. I had a Johnny Velvet poster on my wall when I was in the fourth grade. I was going to marry him. The Vibes were a part of every mix tape I made. So, Johnny Velvet must be the subject of Tish Taylor's next book."

He rolled his eyes and flipped through the items on the conference table. Duncan picked up the DVD and popped it in his laptop.

They spent the morning breezing through news clips and some cheesy interviews and videos that made Delanie nostalgic for the big '80s.

There was one grainy video of an auto accident. Duncan opened the file, and they watched a shiny red sports car flash across the screen and speed down a bridge. The picture tilted and twitched, and a loud noise echoed in the background. The video, a mess of jerky motions, finally righted itself and focused on the roadway and a mountain. They heard muffled shouts that were hard to translate into actual words. The screen went black. After a second or two, the car reappeared. It accelerated toward the cement rails. Then the car jumped the curb, hit one of the pillars, and continued over the side toward the lake. Flames shot skyward until they disappeared with what was left of the red car as it slipped under the water.

"I remember when Johnny Velvet died. This was the video they showed over and over," Delanie said as Duncan replayed the clip. "It pops up like the crash pictures of Jayne Mansfield, James Dean, or Princess Diana… Something's wrong with it. I wonder who shot it."

"People didn't walk around with cellphones then," he said, turning off the video.

"We never see the dead Johnny Velvet in the video. But we get a good view of the Hollywood sign and the mountains in the background."

After a short phone call to the assistant in California, Duncan and Delanie surfed the net for information on Johnny Velvet. The singer's real name was John Bailey. Tod's lead was that Johnny Velvet was alive and living quietly as John Bailey in rural Amelia County, Virginia, a few miles west of Delanie's home base in Chesterfield County. Duncan's search revealed a bunch of John Baileys in Central Virginia, but only one was in the right age range. Tod had also theorized that someone may have tampered with the car and caused the accident that was reported to have killed Johnny Velvet. He had asked that they look at that angle during their search through the facts in the rock star's death.

Delanie finally broke the silence. "So, where's the body?"

"None of the videos show the body being removed from the submerged car. I'll see what I can find."

"If he faked his own death, then it stands to reason that someone paid off the police."

"Hmmm," he said. "There were major LAPD corruption issues back then. It's as good a theory as any."

"Okay, Dunc, we've got a starting point. But we need a plan. I'm going to Amelia County tomorrow to see what I can find. They don't have their public records online yet, so I'll nose around the courthouse. We'll see if Tish Taylor's rumor mill is on the right track. Maybe we can look into the guy who survived the wreck too," Delanie said.

"He's on my list. Are you headed to Amelia County overnight? If you need a room, I can call my Aunt Savannah to see if she has space at the bed and breakfast."

"Right now, it's a day trip. If I have to answer questions, my story is that I'm doing research on family genealogy in Amelia County. That should let me snoop for a while. But could you call your aunt to see if I could stop by for a local perspective? I may want to go back for the weekend or part of next week. We'll see how my first trip goes."

"I'll call her tonight. I'm going to stay here and do some more research. I need to check out the John Bailey leads. One of those interviews mentioned that Johnny Velvet had a child. I'm gonna see what I can find. I want to look at his record label too. You know, if he's still alive and there were insurance claims for his death, Tish might have a fraud angle to go with her 'he's alive' story." Duncan leaned over and scratched Margaret behind the ears. The dog rolled over and flailed all four legs to ensure a tummy rub.

"This could be one of our more interesting cases, and between this and the one for the Treasure Chest, it sure beats stakeouts of cheating spouses. We know Chaz is a sleazy businessman and that's what drives him. But why would Johnny Velvet give up rock stardom for Amelia County, Virginia?"

"Who knows? According to what I've found so far, the Virginia John Bailey inherited his grandparents' farm when his granny died about fifteen years ago. The grandfather died about three months before Johnny Velvet's car crash. The Virginia JB is single and drives an old Ford pickup. He pays his property taxes on the twenty-eight-hundred square foot farmhouse and the two-hundred-fifty acre farm. The property also has a barn and several small outbuildings. He's Methodist and six-foot-five. And he does a lot of shopping on the Internet."

Delanie wondered where Duncan found his information, but she learned long ago not to ask questions as long as he used his powers for good. Packing up the Johnny Velvet box, she said, "Okay, so he had family here. Maybe the childhood farm memories were a draw or maybe he was escaping something in his adult life."

The sun had disappeared during their working session, and her stomach grumbled to let her know the time.

"I'm gonna take this box home. Do you need anything out of it?"

"Nah. I copied the DVD, so you can take it, too," he said, popping the disc out of his laptop and sliding it into the plastic jewel case.

"Thanks for all the background information." She dropped it on top of the other Vibes memorabilia. Gathering up the box and her purse, she stepped over Margaret and headed for the door. "You want me to put the lights on? I'm headed out," she said.

"Just the hall and the kitchen ones will do. Margaret and I are going to hang out here for a while and make some calls. I want to see what else I can find. I'll let you know if I uncover anything interesting." Duncan and Margaret retreated to his office.

Delanie headed out to grab a drive-thru salad and an iced tea and plow through the box again. She locked the front door behind her and headed for the car.

As a young girl, she had pictures of Johnny Velvet and The Vibes all over her walls, and she wrote Delanie Velvet in pink with little hearts over each *i* on all her notebooks. The thought of finding Johnny Velvet alive after all these years thrilled her.

But why rural Virginia? There were famous people from Central Virginia, but most had lived here in their youth and moved away as adults. She hadn't heard of anyone returning to the sticks because they missed the country life. The money and affluence were centered on Charlottesville because of the university, the nearby horse country, and Virginia Beach's oceanfront. Amelia County was a tiny, bucolic spot west of Richmond with a population of a little over twelve thousand. Its big claim to fame was in 1865 as part of Lee's retreat to Appomattox at the end of the Civil War. This county seat was as far from the rock 'n' roll glamour of Los Angeles as you could get. Could a now fifty-year-old Johnny Velvet be hiding in plain sight on a farm?

THREE

DELANIE JUGGLED A breakfast sandwich and a coffee while driving 65 miles an hour on Route 360 West when Chaz called for the second time. She let this one go to voicemail. After reviewing Ami's stories about him, she wasn't too keen on talking to her bad-boy client until she had more to report. His rap sheet was several pages long, and Ami had dug up information from his juvenile days. According to Ami's sources, he liked loose women and fast cars. He came from a privileged family and assumed everything was his for the taking. His father had been an investment banker, and his mother had been a member of the First Families of Virginia, with roots going all the way back to Jamestown. She died of cancer when Chaz was in elementary school, and his father had passed away when Chaz was in college, leaving the sleazy skirt chaser with a fat inheritance. It seemed he had invested most of his money in the Treasure Chest. According to Duncan, his net worth should have been much greater than what his bank accounts and tax assessments showed.

Delanie buried thoughts of Chaz and spent the rest of the ride listening to her Vibes CDs. She hoped she would divine something from the lyrics, but the songs she had been so enamored with in middle school weren't as deep as she remembered.

She turned off the music and took the only exit to Amelia County's business district, passing the tiny country club, a farm insurance company, and a feed and seed store. Right before her turn at the courthouse, she saw a strip mall with a laundromat and a Dollar General. The downtown reminded her of Mayberry from decades ago.

The courthouse area looked like a park. Its antebellum building faced a tree-lined walkway and the obligatory statue, facing south. The courthouse's large portico, supported by four white columns and shaded by oak trees, had probably been here when Lee and the boys in gray marched by. Antique and consignment shops, a bank, and a glass repair service bordered the square. Methodist and Baptist churches bookended the library and the tiny sheriff's office across the street. She saw four people walking around the downtown area and a couple of cars parked near where she idled in the black Mustang. For a county government center, it wasn't that busy.

Parking across from the two antique shops, Delanie followed the small blue signs up the path to the county records department. The bells on the door jangled as she made her way from the sunny square to the dark government building that smelled of lunches eaten at battered government desks and stale air-conditioning.

"May I help you, dear?" asked the clerk, whose hair looked granny blue under the fluorescent lights. The diminutive woman stretched slightly to lean on the Formica counter. Her name tag read *Emmie Rae*, and she was decked out in an aqua and purple muumuu.

"Yes, thank you. I'm doing some research on property titles, wills, and genealogy in Amelia County and the surrounding area. Could you point me to the right place?" Delanie leaned her purple leather purse on the counter that had pink, blue, and tan squiggly marks for decoration.

"Well, I can help you with the titles, property records, and wills. We have an index, and then you look up the code in the deed books. The wills are in that gray cabinet over there. They're indexed by last name. For the genealogy, you're going to have to walk over to the library across the square. They have a county reference section. We charge for copies, but it's free to look through the indices and the deeds, so help yourself. We close at twelve o'clock for lunch. Holler if you need anything."

"Will do." Delanie settled in to peruse the Bailey family information. About eleven forty-five, she noticed that Emmie Rae was making a slight clucking sound and pacing back and forth behind the counter.

Delanie packed up her notes and asked, "Excuse me, where's a good place for lunch?"

"Mason's is the closest. They have lunch there. But there's a McDonald's back on Route 360 a few miles east of here if you want something fancier."

"Where's Mason's?"

"Go across the square and two blocks to the northeast. It's a blue-grey wood building with a red tin roof. It has two old gas pumps with the glass globes out front, but he doesn't sell gasoline anymore. If you came in off of Route 360, you drove right past it. He has a lot of old petroleum signs on the walls."

"Thanks for the directions and all the records." Delanie left her car and walked over.

She didn't have a problem finding Mason's in the downtown that was only about four square blocks. However, Emmie Rae neglected to tell her that Mason's was a combination country store, lunch counter, and bait-taxidermy shop. She grabbed a menu and slid into one of the red vinyl booths. Each of the tiny tables had some example of Mason's animal-stuffing skills. The raccoon at the first table looked rabid with its fangs and glassy eyes. She chose a table with a squirrel, clutching a large walnut.

Despite the décor, Mason's served a pretty good burger and chocolate shake. Delanie wiped the grease off of her fingers and reviewed her notes on the Bailey family of Amelia County before she walked over to the county's library.

She arrived a few minutes before one o'clock to find a closed-for-lunch sign on the door. There were only two or three people eating sandwiches on the park benches. Sitting on the library's cement steps, bordered by long, aluminum railings, she waited for the lunch hour to end.

At a quarter after one, someone opened the door, and Delanie jumped at the chance to get out of the heat. The June afternoon had warmed up way past comfortable, and it was a relief to soak in the air-conditioning. Delanie wandered through the small cinderblock building to the reference section located in the back right corner. The local genealogy society had a gold mine of family files, and someone had diligently documented ten generations of the Bailey family tree, which claimed Thomas Jefferson's father and the great orator, Henry Clay, as relatives. No children were listed for the Virginia John Bailey. In fact, the research ended with his generation, so she couldn't prove either way that he had any descendants. She was disappointed the archives didn't include family photos or letters. She was hoping to find more than what Duncan had found in his search.

Delanie's phone alerted again to a string of texts from Duncan about what he had found. He also noted that Aunt Savannah would be around this afternoon if she wanted to stop in.

Even though it was only a couple of blocks away, Delanie drove to Aunt Savannah's bed and breakfast, the Amelia Sophia, a restored white Victorian. The B&B looked like a dollhouse with its lavender gingerbread work and beautiful English garden, set back from the main road. Delanie followed the pebbled path to the wraparound front porch with lounges and a swing. A few minutes after she rang the bell, Duncan's Aunt Savannah Victoria Jones waddled to the front door.

"Well, I'll be," she said, opening the screened door. "Delanie Lynn, how are you, honey?"

"Fine, Mrs. Jones. Did I catch you at a bad time?" Delanie asked, smiling at the Southern pleasantries.

"No, Duncan said you'd stop by. Let me run in and get us some drinks to quench our thirst on this scorcher of a day. Make yourself comfortable, and I'll be back in a jiff. Lemonade or iced tea?" Duncan's snow-white haired aunt asked.

"Tea is fine, but please don't go to any trouble. I wanted to stop in and see you since I was nearby." Delanie found a cool spot on the porch swing. She got a whiff of lavender when the breeze blew.

Aunt Savannah returned a few minutes later carrying a tray with unsweetened tea and iced cookies. Aunt Savannah added sweetener and a lemon wedge to hers.

"So, what brings you to our fair county?"

"I'm doing some genealogy research on the families who have been here a while, specifically the John Bailey clan. I've been to the records office and the library so far and got the basics for the family. So, what else do I need to know about them that I wouldn't find there?"

Delanie liked Duncan's Aunt Savannah, a Southern lady through and through, who could sweetly dish the dirt on everyone. Her unspoken philosophy was Alice Roosevelt Longworth's quote, "If you don't have anything nice to say, come here and sit beside me."

"WELL, LET'S SEE," Aunt Savannah said as she repositioned the cushions. "Polly and John Tyler Bailey lived in Amelia County for years. They went to the Methodist church. Most of them are buried either out there at the church cemetery or in the family plot on the farm. John Sr. died about twenty-five years ago. Polly, short for Palmyra, kept the farm. Her grandson, John III, moved here in the nineties to help out. Polly's son, John Jr., moved his family to California years ago for work, but the current John used to spend summer vacations here. I think he was an only child. John Jr. did something with the military or the government on the West Coast. Polly passed on a while back, and I guess the youngest of the Johns decided to stay here after her death. I don't know what happened to his parents. I don't remember them ever coming to visit."

"Where is the Bailey farm?" Delanie asked, reaching for a lemon snap.

"It's about eight miles from here. Take Route 681. Just past the Veteran's Cemetery, Pridesville Road turns into Clementown Road, and it's about a mile up on the right. It's called Summerford. There's a fairly large white sign at the edge of the road. The driveway winds through a lot of trees to a house that's set back from the road. You'll see the sign before you see the house. It's been in the Bailey family since the early eighteen hundreds, so it's got historic status."

"How well did you know the family?"

"I went to high school with Polly and John Tyler. We also went to church together. Her grandson only darkens the door on Easter or Christmas. I don't see him around much. He's pretty quiet, and he goes to the library from time to time. I hear he also frequents Billie's. It tries to be a nightclub, but it's really a honky tonk, and it's about the only place around to drink or dance unless you head back toward Richmond."

"I don't remember seeing it when I drove in."

"You must have blinked. It's an old building with a tin roof next to the Dollar General. They have karaoke and line dancing. They serve dinner too in hopes of appealing to more regular folks, but it just attracts the rowdies on the weekends."

"What about the younger John Bailey, the grandson? What did he do in California before he moved back here?"

"I don't rightly know. Polly would talk about him coming to visit, but I don't remember her mentioning anything about his life in California. She never talked much about her son or grandson."

"Have you seen him lately? Anything unique about his appearance?"

"Nope on both accounts. He's tall, and he dresses like all the other men around here. Nothing special."

"Thank you so much for the refreshments and the information. I appreciate your help. If I come back later next week, do you have a room available?"

"Honey, I always have room for you. Just give me a call. Bring Duncan out with you next time. I haven't seen him in eons. He stays indoors too much. He's way too pale. I don't know what I'm going to do with that boy. We need to find him a nice girl."

"Will do. Thanks again. The iced tea hit the spot. I'll see you again soon." Delanie hugged Duncan's aunt.

DELANIE FOUND SUMMERFORD EASILY. Driving past slowly, she turned around and idled back to the property, surrounded by farmland. She pulled in the driveway and shoved her notes under the front seat. Delanie shut off the car and walked around outside. She was blocking the gravel driveway. The white farmhouse sat about five hundred yards ahead with a red barn off in the distance. Either side of the driveway was surrounded by a copse of trees, but it looked like the woods thinned out closer to the house.

She leaned down near the Mustang's back tire, working up her flat tire ruse if anyone appeared. With older cars, she would have to let some air out. Now with all the electronics, it was easy to claim that the sensor went off. Delanie walked around the car a couple of times. She delayed her decision to walk toward the farmhouse when she noticed someone on a four-wheeler coming her way.

Delanie hurried back to the tire and squatted. The guy pulled up next to her and shut off the motor.

He didn't speak until the dust and rocks settled. Jumping off the brown vehicle, he asked, "Hey. What's the problem?" Delanie could hear the engine ticking in the sudden stillness.

"I'm sorry to bother you. I was going to call AAA, but I can't get a signal out here. My back tire sensor went off. It doesn't look flat, but I wanted to call someone to check it before I head back to Richmond."

"It'll take a while to get someone out here. Do you want me to look at it? I've got an air compressor in the barn."

"Thank you. I appreciate your help. I didn't mean to disturb anyone. I'm Delanie."

"Hi, Delanie. I'm John." She tried to get a good look at his face. John was tall with sandy blond hair and piercing blue eyes. Johnny Velvet had blue eyes, but much darker hair. John's face was rugged, but he wore the wrinkles well. Dressed in a white T-shirt, blue jeans, and work boots, he looked like a Southern farmer who preferred country music to rock 'n' roll.

Delanie remembered Johnny Velvet with long, dark brown hair and leather pants. If they were the same person, he was a far cry from the big-haired, flamboyant rocker of the '80s. She thought she'd be able to recognize him, but the voice didn't sound familiar.

"Do you have a tire gauge?" he asked, leaning over to look at the back tire.

"I might." She leaned in through the driver's side

to check the glove box. "What do ya know? I do," she said, flipping it to him.

He poked the tire and checked the chart on the inside of the door. "It's a little low, but not bad. If you want to drive it to the barn, I'll top it off. You should be good to go for the rest of your trip." He wiped the tire gauge on his shirttail and handed it back to her.

"Thanks." She followed him down the dusty driveway past the white house to the barn. He opened two large, wooden doors and waved her in. She rolled in, thinking of horror movies in out-of-the-way settings.

Delanie shook off the creepy feeling and pulled in next to a work area on the right. John dragged the compressor around to her side of the car after she shut off the engine. Tools neatly outlined the perimeter of the workspace. The hay smell tickled her nose.

She climbed out while he topped off the tire. Something moved in the back of the barn and reared up. She could see it on the other side of the car through the passenger door window. It looked like a six-foot Muppet with a bad reddish perm. She screamed and fell over backwards in her attempt to retreat. The thing squealed and trotted to the back of the barn.

"What's wrong?" John asked, dropping the compressor hose.

"I'm not sure," she said, standing up and wiping the dust and hay off her jeans. "I saw something on the other side of the car, and it shrieked at me."

"That's Myrtle."

"Myrtle?"

He whistled. "Delanie, this is Myrtle, the alpaca. Her

boyfriend Stewart is in the paddock." On cue, Myrtle returned to sniff Delanie and the car.

"Nice to meet you, Myrtle. Sorry if I startled you." Delanie put out her hand. The alpaca sniffed her hand and hair and let Delanie pet her head.

"She's usually friendly and a tad nosy… There, the car should be ready to go."

"Thank you so much. I appreciate the help, and I'm sorry to intrude on your afternoon."

"That should hold you 'til you get back to town. Get the warning checked out if it comes on again," he said, wiping his hands on his jeans.

"Will do. I'll see you around. Bye, Myrtle."

John nodded, and Delanie backed out and turned around in the yard. Her knees still felt wobbly from Myrtle the alpaca's dramatic entrance, but she felt good about the first visit. And she definitely would be seeing John around. He just didn't know it yet.

She'd have to get pictures or DNA next time. The tire gauge he wiped down wasn't going to work. At first glance, Delanie wasn't sold that John Bailey was Johnny Velvet. People change a lot over the years. But nothing around here indicated that he was once a teen heartthrob.

Back on the main road, she cranked up the stereo with her Vibes CD to see if this John sounded anything at all like Johnny Velvet. It was hard to compare the singing voice to the guy who checked her tire. Delanie needed to work on a story to wheedle her way back to Summerford and John Bailey.

FOUR

DELANIE GLANCED AT the dash clock before she backed out of her gravel driveway. It read *8:18*. She might still catch Duncan before World of Warcraft night; he never missed video game sessions.

She glanced at her house with the sun going down behind it. Though small, her bungalow was the right size for her, and it had character. Delanie loved her 1939 kit house, ordered from a Sears catalog. The chimney was the prominent feature of the Yates' model, with its white triangular front and archway over the front door. She loved the floorboards and beams throughout the house, some labeled with model and catalog numbers. The yard was old enough to have established trees.

"Hey," Duncan said, answering Delanie's phone call. Interrupting her thoughts, his voice came through her car radio.

"Sorry to bother you on WOW night. I wanted to know if you found anything else on our John Bailey of Virginia."

"Where're you off to?"

"It's line dancing and karaoke night at Billie's. I'm hoping to run into our JB and make it look like an unplanned coincidence."

"Well, I found some interesting things. Johnny Velvet does indeed have a child who grew up in Chicago.

The mom was a television personality when she met Johnny of The Vibes. She was a talking head on one of those television gossip shows. Her name was Kelly Mercer, but she was born Kelly Ann Henderson in Marion, Wisconsin."

"Intriguing," Delanie said. A chicken truck passed her going in the opposite direction. She put up her window to avoid the feathers that were floating in the truck's wake. Delanie knew where the chickens were going. Poor things. The thought was almost enough to make her want to become vegetarian. "What about the child?" she asked.

"She would be in her twenties by now. I don't think she knew Johnny V. Her mom split with her and headed for Chicago when the kid was itty-bitty. Her name is Emily Jane Mercer. She's been in the Windy City ever since."

"We should make contact. I'll start with the mom."

"That's the wrinkle. A drunk driver killed Kelly Mercer in 1995. Emily Jane ended up living with her grandmother."

"Okay, see if you can track down the grandma. While you're poking around, follow the money. Any insurance claims or child support?"

"Working on it," he said. "I'll let you know if I unravel anything. Are you staying in Amelia County tonight?"

"No. I don't plan to hang around that long. I'll probably make an appearance at the office later tomorrow."

"Me too. And don't have too much fun. You're supposed to be working."

"I won't have any fun, and I'm definitely working."

"Hey, my monsters are virtual, and I can always turn off the game and go back to real life. You can't, so be careful. I'll see you tomorrow. I left you a folder on Chaz's mortal enemy list. It indeed looks like the mayor's friends are ganging up on him, though it's kind of hard to feel sorry for him." Duncan took a long breath.

"Thanks, you're great! Give Margaret a hug for me. See ya tomorrow," Delanie said, pushing the button to disconnect the phone.

A little after nine, Delanie pulled into the small lot in front of the Dollar General. Billie's was a cinderblock building with a wooden front porch and a tin roof that had been painted red long ago. The smallish building at the edge of the parking lot had seen better days.

Delanie wandered in and found an empty stool. About twenty people sat at tables and booths around the bar. A DJ stood in the corner, and a few nodded appreciation of his tune. They were line dancing to an old Brooks and Dunn song that Delanie liked.

The bartender stopped twirling her corkscrew curls. "Hey, welcome to Billie's. What can I get you?"

"Ginger ale to start, please," Delanie said, balancing on a leatherette barstool that rocked slightly when she moved.

"New in town?" the bartender asked as she put the drink on a red napkin.

"Sort of. I'm doing some research around the county for an article I'm writing. And I'll be in and out of town for the next few weeks. I wanted to get a taste of the nightlife."

"Here it is," she said. The bartender laughed and waved her arms. "We're the only place in town, if you don't count the Moose Lodge. We have karaoke on Tuesday and a band on the weekend."

"Thanks, how much?" Delanie asked, pointing to her glass.

"Don't worry about it. We'll start counting when you have something stronger."

Delanie nodded and dropped a five in a tip jar that looked as if it had once been home to pickles.

The bartender moved on to fill an order for a waitress wearing a fringed Western shirt and cut-off shorts with white boots. The line-dancing group moved on to another song, and a few guys in the back surrounded the single pool table near some risers that served as a small stage.

After her third ginger ale and a trip to the little cowgirls' room, Delanie was getting ready to call it a bust. She turned to slide off the stool and realized two guys had materialized on either side of her.

"Hi," said the one in jeans and a plaid shirt as he leaned into her space. His slicked-back dark hair with sideburns reminded Delanie of an anemic Elvis. His belt buckle, the size of a dessert plate, looked like something a professional wrestler might wear.

"Hey," said the second guy with a jagged scar that ran from the corner of his mouth to the base of his chin. She wondered what caused such a mark, but she didn't want to prolong the conversation by asking.

"Hello," Delanie said. She slid off the stool and pointed her toes toward the exit at the front of the bar.

"I'm Ricky. You leaving already? It's way too early to be going home. The fun hasn't started yet," the guy with the scar said.

His side-burned friend said, "I'm Dallas. And you are?"

"I've got an early morning. It's nice to meet you both," she said, taking a few steps toward the exit.

"Ricky, I don't think she's interested in our company," Dallas said. He bumped into the barstool, and it wobbled while he talked.

"I've got to go to work tomorrow. Y'all have fun." Delanie flipped her purse strap over her shoulder.

Ricky nodded and turned to order from the bartender. Delanie dodged chairs on her way to the front door.

Lampposts near the building provided a soft glow, but their haloed lights faded quickly as she walked deeper into the lot. Pulling her purse closer, she reached in for her keys and closed her fingers around the pepper spray Duncan left her as a present last Christmas.

As she closed in on her car, Delanie heard a noise behind her. She sped up, but all she could hear were footsteps crunching on the gravel.

"Hey, wait!" Dallas yelled. He slid to a stop next to her beside several older pickup trucks.

"What?"

"It's way too early. I think you should come back in and have at least one drink with us. And we're pretty good dancers," slurred the cowboy with his shirttail hanging out. Dallas was about five-foot-seven. She had her throw-me-down dance shoes on, and she towered over him by three or four inches.

"I appreciate it. I really do, but I've got to get up early for work tomorrow. I need to take a rain check." She turned to move, and he clamped down on her arm.

In one swift move, Delanie flipped her purse back over her shoulder and aimed the pepper spray, legs spread and knees bent as if she held a revolver. Before she could douse him, someone said, "Hey, Cowboy, I don't think the lady's interested." She turned to see who her protector was.

John Bailey had Dallas by the collar, making the shorter guy balance on his tiptoes.

Dallas sputtered, but nothing coherent came out. John let go, and Dallas landed with a thump on his backside. He rolled over, swearing and muttering. He stood and staggered back to the bar, wiping the dust and loose gravel from the back of his jeans as he walked.

"John, is it? It's nice to run into you again. And thanks for the assistance again," she said, trying to act like it was a spontaneous meeting. "I'm not always the damsel in distress. You probably think I'm trouble by now."

"Not a problem. He needed to be reminded of his manners," John said. She noticed his crisp jeans and red shirt, but there was nothing reminiscent of Johnny Velvet.

"I was getting to that. Kind of sad I didn't get to make him cry," Delanie said, putting her pepper spray back in her purse. "Uh, can I buy you a drink?"

"Looks like you were leaving. Wanna get coffee instead? You probably don't want to go back in there with that Bubba. I know a place up on the highway that has great pie."

"Well, that clinches it. How can I say no to great pie? I'll follow you."

A few minutes later, she turned left into the Isle of Capri parking lot. It was an old house with a stone facade that had been reinvented as an Italian restaurant. The neon sign in the front window flashed that they were open. She parked next to John's truck, and they walked in through what was the previous house's front door.

After the waitress took their order, John asked, "So what brings you to Billie's and our fair Amelia County?"

"I'm working on an article on some of the families from the area. I thought I'd stop in and soak up the local color."

"Looks like you got to see some of the quality folks tonight."

Delanie smiled. The waitress brought her lemon pie and John's slice of pecan pie along with two cups of coffee. "Interesting place. You go there often?"

"Once in a while. It's about the only place around unless you head east to Chesterfield County or Richmond."

"Did you grow up here?"

"Nah," he said, digging into his pie. "I spent summers here with my grandparents when I was a kid. I grew up in sunny, funny California."

"The West Coast sounds much more exciting and warmer. I have to ask, why'd you leave?"

"You from here?"

"Chesterfield County," she said, trying not to talk with a mouthful of lemon meringue.

"California's okay, but it was time to make a change. My grandparents were ill, so the pull to move back home was stronger than anything holding me there," he said, stirring his coffee. "I was between jobs and nothing on the Left Coast looked promising. Plus, I guess I wanted a new start. When my grandfather died, I decided to move here to help my grandmother with the farm."

"I think I would like to live in a big city somewhere. Richmond still has a small town feel," she said, looking closely at him. She was trying to decide if she thought he was really Johnny Velvet. Some of the timelines could be falling into place, but she wasn't convinced. *If Duncan aged a Johnny Velvet photo, would it look anything like John Bailey?*

"It's not all that it's cracked up to be. I traveled a lot, but it's nice to settle down sometimes."

"On a farm with Myrtle," she said, smiling.

"And Stewart and Dolly the donkey. There are also five dogs, four barn cats, six goats, and a bunch of chickens."

"You've got your own menagerie."

"Hey, they do fill the barn. It's quiet out there most of the time except if I'm late with dinner," he said, finishing off his pie.

The waitress brought the check, and John took it before Delanie could reach for it.

"Are you sure? It's the least I can do for the tire repair and the muscle with Dallas."

He smiled. "If you're ever back this way, let me know, and maybe we could go to dinner."

"That would be nice." She reached in her purse for a pen and wrote her name and number on a paper napkin.

She handed it to John when he returned from paying the tab. He folded the napkin and put it in his shirt pocket.

When they stopped next to her car, he asked, "You can get back all right from here?"

"Sure, it's pretty much a straight shot down Route 360. Thanks for the coffee and pie and all the help."

He waited for her to back out before he climbed in his truck.

That almost felt like a real date even though I'm technically stalking him for Tish Taylor's next book.

FIVE

DELANIE FINISHED FILING a broken nail before she reached for the jangling office phone. "Hey, Robbie," she said, balancing the headset on her shoulder while continuing to file. "'Bout time you called your baby sister." Robbie, a bouncer at the trendy Club Echo, kept different hours than the rest of the world.

"Sorry, but you know I work six days a week, and I met someone recently." It sounded to Delanie that he was calling from his car with the windows down.

"So, do I get to meet this one or is she another Miss Right Now?"

"Very funny. You're one to talk. Are you dating anyone, or are your dates still pretend because you're stalking them?"

"Hey, I stalk for a living," she said, working on the nails on the other hand.

"Okay, so what's new with you? Anything fun or has it been just all work?" asked Robbie, the athletic sibling. He had a baseball stint in the minor leagues until he blew out his knee, ruining his chances of ever being called up to the MLB.

"One of my new clients is a neighbor of yours, and I wanted to get the buzz on him. His name is Charles Wellington Smith, the third."

"Oh, Chaz. Run away fast. He's an idiot. Whatever

you do, don't take the job. He's been in and out of jail since high school. He's a trust-fund baby who tries to be a big shot. But I'm guessing, you've already taken the job, haven't you?"

"Uh huh. He seemed okay. He's having trouble getting permits from the city for the new business he wants to open."

"It's a strip club he wants to put in the middle of the Museum district. He's not popular with respectable folks. Most people avoid him like the plague." Before Delanie could comment, her brother continued. "He thinks he's a badass. He throws money around and always has to be the center of attention. He got that stupid face tattoo when he was in juvie jail. I don't think he ever killed anyone. He's just trying to look tough and to gain street cred without having to do anything. Be careful. He doesn't bring out the best in others."

"I will. You worry too much. It seems like an interesting job, but I'll be doubly careful."

"When he goes downtown, he always shows up with a posse. They drive around in a caravan, led by that tacky Hummer. He always travels in a pack, and he likes to make a scene."

"He seems like a colorful guy."

"Just remember that I'm the cool brother. If Steve finds out you're working for Chaz, you'll never hear the end of it."

Steve, their oldest brother and protector since both parents had passed away, doubled as a Chesterfield County police officer. Robbie was right. Steve would give little sis Delanie unending grief about working with Chaz.

"Hopefully, Chaz will be out of my life in a week or so, and it'll be a fascinating story by the time I talk to Lieutenant Steve."

"Wishful thinking. Chaz is like a bad penny. Hey, if you're downtown, stop in and see me. I got a new couch and a lamp."

"Real furniture? I'll definitely come for a visit soon now that there's a place to sit. And thanks for all the information. See ya soon, and maybe I get to meet the new girlfriend too?" If she were like any of the previous ones, she'd be replaced before Delanie made it downtown for a visit.

She clicked off and picked up Duncan's thick folder on Chaz. The "I Hate Chaz" club had recruited quite a few members. She immersed herself in Duncan's notes about her new, unusual client.

The phone jarred her back to reality. "Falcon Investigations."

"Hey, Delanie. This is Chaz. How're things?"

"Good. I've got some information for you."

Before she could finish her thought, he interrupted with, "Well, email it, and we can look at it together."

"I'd rather not. It includes all kinds of stuff that probably shouldn't be floating around on the Internet."

"It's probably out there already, but okay. Can you meet me in a little while? How about El Tigre at the Main Street Station?"

She agreed and let out a long sigh when he clicked off. She didn't know if she could muster the energy to deal with Chaz.

Almost an hour and a half later, Delanie looped around the block for the third time looking for a parking spot.

It was after the lunch rush, but parking was still at a premium. Spotting someone leaving, she jumped in his space.

Delanie found Chaz waiting for her in a booth in the front of the chichi restaurant in the restored train station. He was shoveling small appetizers into his mouth with the fervor of someone who hadn't eaten all day. At his current pace, the plate would be empty before Delanie joined him.

"Hello," she said. She slid in the booth across from him.

He nodded, not interrupting his pace. He finally said, "Whatcha got?"

She pushed a black folder across the table to him. He didn't move except to eat. "Well, Mr. McDermott of the homeowners association is indeed friends with the mayor and his wife. It seems you irritated him with your graffiti stunt, and he and the association have declared war. They filed complaints with the city that include gripes about everything from the noise to lewd behavior in public. We were able to confirm that they're targeting your current location, as well as the new site."

He swallowed and gulped down half a glass of beer. He stopped eating long enough to pick his nose with his index finger.

Delanie diverted her eyes and tried not to gag. She started formulating excuses for not shaking hands with him. She regained her composure.

"Their squeaky wheels seem to be getting the grease. Police presence is up around your club, and the traffic department is looking at redefining the on-street parking around both of your properties. And it's not just the city. You may not get a liquor license because the ABC board had multiple complaints about a series of violations at your current establishment."

"We're a strip club. We follow most of the rules, but we aren't dealing with choirboys. A lot of my clientele aren't strangers to the police. Hell, a couple of 'em *are* the police. You want anything to eat?"

"No thanks. But they're not targeting your clients specifically. They're looking at your alcohol-versus-food sales, number of police visits, and allegations of drug and alcohol violations and underage drinking. You need to talk to an attorney. You're under a lot of scrutiny, and if one or two of the complaints come to fruition, you and your business could be in jeopardy. Your enemy list is quite long."

"Rumor on the street is that our righteous and upstanding mayor has a thing on the side," Chaz said, wiping his mouth on his sleeve. "I want to get some details. I want to be able to show that he's a hypocrite and his Mr. Squeaky Clean image has some cracks in it. He keeps throwing stones at me, but he's like the rest of us."

"This is a little out of the scope of the jobs we normally investigate," Delanie said. "Falcon Investigations usually does workman's comp or divorce cases." Delanie wondered where this allegation came from. It sounded like Chaz was trying to change the subject to deflect some of his problems.

"Think of this as a pre-divorce case, which it might be if Mrs. Mayor is hip to any of this. It's righting an injustice. You'd be helping the underdog. Come on, Delanie, you know they're singling me out and targeting my business. If they can do it to me, they can do it to anyone. Come on. You know what it's like to be a small business owner."

He wasn't quite the sympathetic underdog, but Delanie didn't try to explain this fact to him. She pretended to weigh his request for help in getting dirt on the mayor. Before she could decline, Chaz slid a white envelope across the table and said, "Here, this should cover a week's worth of checking into things. Let me know if it's going to cost me more."

Before Delanie could pick up the envelope, a tall woman approached the table. Dressed in a tight leopard-print micro dress, she wore enough makeup for an all-day photo shoot. She stopped at their table and transferred a large Coach bag to her other shoulder. Her arm was covered in bangle bracelets that clinked when she moved. The tight dress and the big hair were enough to cause stares, but the opening in the front of the dress could stop traffic. It looked like she was only moments away from a wardrobe malfunction. Delanie wasn't sure how the woman balanced all that buoyancy on those four-inch stilettos.

"Well, lookie who's here," she said to Chaz. "I haven't seen you in a while. You too big to return calls now?"

"We don't have anything else to talk about," he said. "And if you'll excuse us, I'm trying to conduct some business here."

The woman who filled every inch of the dress shifted her weight. Delanie feared she might topple forward into the pile of dirty plates. She made a harrrrumpf sound. "Well, I have something to say to you. I was one of the loyal ones, and now you don't even return my calls. Chaz, you're a shit. You owe me, and you're going to pay one way or the other. You wouldn't know a good thing if it bit you on the ass," she said, waving her arms in large circles.

By then, guests at nearby tables and some of the wait staff stopped to watch. Before anyone could reply, she continued in a higher octave with, *"Yoooou are definitely going to be sorry. I know things. You don't get to just dismiss people."* She turned and stomped off to the delight of the diners and a gaggle of waiters. Delanie was surprised that no one applauded or took photographs.

Chaz made no comment about the drama. Delanie cleared her throat and said, "Well, Mr. Smith. There's enough here to cover us looking into your allegations about the mayor. I'll be in touch in a few days with what we find. I wouldn't leave this folder lying around. It has some details that you might not want to share," she said, pushing the shiny black folder closer. "Oh, and what's her name? I probably should add it to your list."

"She goes by Cherri Bomb," he said. "Her real name is Michelle... Michelle Hudson, I think. Yep, that's it. Thanks for the information you've found so far." The embossed gold falcon on the cover of the black folder glimmered under the restaurant's pendant lights. Chaz signaled the waiter for another beer.

Delanie's exit didn't draw the attention that Cherri's did, and thanks to all those hours in Zumba class, she didn't jiggle or wobble as much either.

SIX

DELANIE SLID INTO her red plastic seat as the Richmond Flying Squirrels took the field for stretches. She had been surprised when John Bailey called and asked her to meet him at the local baseball diamond.

"You want something to eat?"

She wedged her small purse between her hip and the armrest. "I'm good for now, thanks." John signaled to the concession guy.

Out of the corner of her eye, Delanie saw Mayor Ed Hunter and his entourage fill a box near the first base line. He and his folks, in suits and ties, were overdressed for the muggy summer evening at the ballpark. She didn't see Mrs. Mayor, so this must be some sort of business outing. Easy to spot with his thick white hair, Mayor Hunter had two guys on either side of him and a few more suits in the seats behind him. There were no women in his crowd.

John settled in and munched on popcorn while Delanie watched the mayor and his group. After the national anthem, the announcer introduced the mayor and several CEOs from local businesses. The mayor stood and waved one hand at the crowd. It was the wave politicians and royalty have perfected.

John was quiet this evening. He had said more to the ticket taker and the drink guy than to her so far.

She wondered if she would be able to worm any information from him this evening. Normally, she wouldn't have much in common with a stoic date, but this guy intrigued her. It was kind of fun to think that she could be on a date with Johnny Velvet.

Nothing was going on in Mayor Hunter's area either. At the bottom of the second inning, all the inhabitants of the box put on red Flying Squirrels caps and made their way to the field, where the mayor welcomed some new CEO to Richmond and congratulated the baseball team for their great season so far. Thankfully, the speech was short, and the game resumed. The ball caps came off as soon as the group left the field, and the players took their places.

Delanie looked at John. "I need a pit stop. I'll be back in a minute. Do you want me to get anything from concessions?"

"I'm set for now. See you in a few."

Climbing the cement stairs, Delanie caught up with the mayor's crowd. She snapped a couple of pictures with her phone. She hoped that Duncan could determine who was in the mayor's entourage. She tried to hear what they were talking about, but the crowd noise drowned out the men's voices.

At the top of the steps, the mayor's party ducked down a gray hallway between two concession stands. Delanie tailed them to the corner. The industrial-looking hallway was empty except for the dignitaries. Hanging out on her side of the wall, she waited until they exited through the third door on the left. When the hall emptied, Delanie jogged down to where they disappeared. The windowless industrial door was marked *2153* on a red plastic plaque. Not hearing anything inside, she walked past the room. Delanie turned the doorknob of the next door, and it opened. Inside, she found a janitorial closet stacked to the ceiling with cleaning supplies. Slipping inside, Delanie tried to hear through the shared wall.

Having no success, she left the custodian's closet. Blending in with the concession crowd, she found a spot with a good vantage of the room. She emailed the photos to Duncan and finished an iced tea and a hot dog before the door opened. Mayor Hunter's team made its way toward her and the stadium's front entrance.

The mayor and his guys shook hands with the executives and their entourages. After some chitchat, Delanie watched them climb into black SUVs idling at the curb at the bottom of the cement steps.

She debated about following them, but she didn't want to duck out on John. She had already been gone a long time. Delanie bought a pretzel and two waters in case he wanted a snack.

Returning to the stands, Delanie was surprised to find John's seat empty. It was the bottom of the seventh inning. After fifteen minutes, she checked her phone to find Duncan had texted her twice about Chaz's case.

John returned during Delanie's chat with Duncan. "Hey. A peace offering." She held up the pretzel and the bottle of water. "Sorry it took so long."

"I was getting concerned. I figured you ditched me." He smiled.

"No way. I got a phone call, and then the line for the women's room snaked out around the concessions."

He didn't explain where he was, and Delanie wondered for a minute if he had followed her.

SEVEN

DELANIE PARKED ON a side street in Richmond's historic Fan District. The row of small businesses merged with townhouses in this quaint part of the city that used to be the original trendy section before the money pushed westward. Delanie walked down the street beside rows of brick buildings with brightly colored awnings and wrought ironwork. On the sidewalk, Delanie stepped around two metal boxes for free newspapers. Ami's *Essence Weekly* was the one on top.

Delanie found Freeda's, a local nightclub, but the front was dark and the door locked. Walking around to the alley behind, she counted buildings until she found the back of Freeda's, renowned for its food and drag show brunches on Sundays. Women came from miles around to drink Freeda's famous pink cocktails and watch the show. The bar boasted a different clientele on the other days of the week.

Finding the green door ajar, Delanie knocked and entered. She wandered down the dark hallway. The lights washed the wooden bar in a warm glow. A bald bear of a man stacked cases and boxes behind the bar.

"Excuse me. I'm looking for Deke Jennings."

"You may have found him," he said as he straightened up. He was a lot taller than she expected, and his dark T-shirt stretched across his biceps.

"I'm Delanie Fitzgerald. Ami Lawrence from *Essence Weekly* gave me your name. She told me that I should speak with you."

"What can I do for you?" he asked hesitantly.

"I have some questions about one of your regulars."

"Reporter?" he asked, unloading bottles under the bar.

"No. Private investigator."

"What do you want to know?" he asked without looking up. "I usually have no comment for reporters, PIs, and cops. However, Ami's a good friend, and you can't be that bad if she sent you. Whatcha need?"

"Thanks," Delanie said with a half-smile. "Rumor on the street has it that a key someone in the very conservative mayor's office is a regular here."

"Maybe. Who're we talking about?"

"Cooper Richardson, the mayor's personal assistant."

"And confidant."

"I thought he was a conservative Republican."

Deke wiped down the counter. After a pause, he replied, "We all have different facets. Some have more freedom to be themselves than others. I dunno, maybe he needed the job? In my opinion, hiding doesn't help anything, but not everybody feels that way."

"Does his significant-other come in with him to the club?" she asked. Deke moved on to arranging the drink prep for tonight's crowd.

"Are you kidding?" He looked at her funny. "Cooper has a patron or a sugar daddy or whatever you want to call the guy who doesn't want to admit what he is. His friend lives in his fancy house with his wife and his perfect life. Appearances are everything to him. He's had powerful jobs in his political party for years. Shoot, his daughter is married to a congressman who's on Fox News every other day or so. The mayor's in denial. I guess he eases his guilt, if he has any, by throwing money at Cooper."

"Anything else you care to share?" Delanie asked.

"Not everything is what it seems. And not everyone tells the truth."

"Thank you for your time and the information. I appreciate it," Delanie said.

"Hey, if you're interested in Cooper Richardson, come back tonight about eleven."

"Around eleven. Why?"

"He keeps a pretty regular schedule. He'll be here. And say hello to Ami for me."

"Thanks again. I'll show myself out," she said, walking back to the alley.

Before getting in the Mustang, she picked up the latest edition of Ami's *Essence Weekly*. She wondered what she would find if she came back tonight looking for the mayor's assistant.

DUNCAN SCRAMBLED OUT of Delanie's car and glared at her. The pair walked down an alley to Freeda's.

"Dunc, I'll make it up to you. I promise. There was no other way. I really need to get some information out of this lead, and it was short notice. You know I appreciate all of your help."

"Don't you have any other guy friends? You could have taken one of your gal pals. Shoot, you could have come by yourself."

"No, I think I'd stand out more as a single female.

I was hoping this would look like I was with a date. Maybe like we wandered in by accident?"

"What about Paisley?" he continued. "You could have brought her. It would have looked more believable with her."

"She's one of my dearest friends, but she talks way too much to be with me when I need to do some under-cover work. Duncan, I really need your help. It won't take long, and I'll buy you a few drinks. Everything will be fine. You'll be home before Margaret misses you."

"Why do I let you talk me into things? And this out-fit! This is so not me," he complained, looking down at his dark jacket and dress pants.

"You look nice. This is what people wear when they go out to clubs. It's not video game night," she said, pointing him toward Freeda's. "You can't wear jeans and T-shirts all the time."

"It's not me. I want it noted that I'm doing this under protest. You're going to have to do something to make up for this. I'll add it to the list," he said, whipping out his phone.

She opened the glass door and grabbed his outstretched hand. The lobby's lounge looked more like a law firm with its burgundy leather chairs and oriental rugs than it did a nightclub. Delanie paid the cover for both of them, and Duncan stood so close that she could feel his breath on her neck.

Feeling a little conspicuous as the only female in the place, she made a show of holding Duncan's hand.

Inside, the bar looked fancier with its artsy pendant lights casting a mellow glow around the perimeter. The ambiance was much more festive tonight than when she had seen it in the off hours. Two Nordic-looking guys in tight, black shirts manned the long bar. She didn't see Deke anywhere on the floor.

Delanie found a table in the corner, and Duncan plopped down in a chair with his back to the majority of the bar's patrons. Before either could speak, a waiter, dressed in black with spiked jet hair and an assortment of piercings asked, "New in town?" Without waiting for a response, he continued with, "You must be. What will you all have?"

"Ginger ale."

"And for you?" the waiter asked, pointing to Duncan.

"Bud in a bottle."

The waiter nodded and returned to the bar area.

"Come on. Cheer up, Duncan. This isn't so bad. This place is nice, and the music's good."

Duncan didn't say a word. He gave her a half-smile and retreated to his phone.

"I'll be right back," she said, picking up her purse. Duncan had a panicked look for a second, but he returned to his phone.

She slid up to the bar at the end close to a table where Cooper Richardson and several friends were sharing drinks and appetizers. The bartender nodded, and she ordered a glass of white wine.

After a couple of sips, she turned to the table where the four men were laughing. "Excuse me. Do I know you?" she asked as she singled out Cooper with a nod and a direct look.

"I don't think so," he said. His friends snickered. "You don't come here often, do you?"

"No, I stopped in with my friend," she said, nodding

toward Duncan. "I thought I saw you with the Mayor at the Richmond Squirrels game last week."

"Yep. I was there for work."

"Well, it's nice to see you again. I didn't mean to interrupt," she said, sliding off her barstool and waving as she headed back to her table with her wineglass.

"About ready?" Duncan asked without looking up from his phone.

"No, just a little while longer. I got video of the folks at his table. I want to see what happens. Maybe you can identify these guys like you did with the Mayor's team at the baseball game. You're a wealth of information."

He nodded and returned to his phone.

Nobody in the bar acted like they noticed Duncan or Delanie. People came and went from Cooper's table all evening, and he left about one-thirty with two other guys. She nudged Duncan, and they followed the three men out of the club.

The other two guys climbed in a dark car parked up the block. Cooper unlocked an older red Porsche and roared away toward Broad Street.

Duncan sulked all the way to the car and plopped down in the passenger seat.

"What is wrong with you? You're in a mood."

"I got dressed up for nothing," he said, shrugging his shoulders.

"Seriously, Duncan. You didn't want to go to the bar, and now you're miffed because no one noticed you?"

EIGHT

DELANIE CAREFULLY PUT the large gift basket filled with Virginia specialties and tied with a big red bow into the passenger seat of the Mustang. Her baseball date with John Bailey was weird, so she wanted to drop off a thank you gift. And maybe she would get the opportunity to learn some more tidbits before she sent another report to Tish Taylor's office. She had hoped that the basket might get her a glimpse inside the white farmhouse. She and Duncan worked all weekend on their research and report, but they didn't come up with much new.

She pulled the door shut and headed for Amelia County. When she left suburbia for the rural landscape, her phone rang. She turned down the volume on her radio and said, "Hi, Ami. What's up?"

"How did you like Deke?"

"He wasn't what I expected. It was like talking to a linebacker. I got a stiff neck trying to look him in the eye. We had an interesting conversation though. He didn't have any earth-shattering news, but he confirmed some suspicions. And he told me when to swing by to see Cooper at the bar. So, what do you know about Cooper Richardson and his mentor?"

"Rumors have swirled around Mayor Hunter for years that he has a thing on the side. No woman has ever come forward. And no one around him has ever made a big deal about it until recently. It seems he's been on a family-values kick for the last few years, which raised eyebrows in some circles. Let's just say some folks in the know don't like the hypocrisy."

"Deke made several comments in that vein," Delanie said, passing a minivan near the farmers market. "Have you all ever done a story on it?"

"Nah, our previous managing editor didn't want to make waves in the city. Ed Hunter held some powerful positions before mayor. Plus, he has friends everywhere. Being mayor seemed to be his quiet retirement job. We're under new management now, so maybe it's time to bring it up again. And there's another year until he's up for re-election. It would definitely be a different angle to the story than the one his camp puts out. You might be on to something. Keep me in the loop with what you find."

"Will do," Delanie said. "And I appreciate, yet again, all of your help. Now, I have to figure out what I want to share with my client."

"Good luck and be careful. Chaz is not the poster boy for discreet. Bye," she said, clicking off.

Delanie made the turn into John Bailey's Summerford. This time she drove down the gravel driveway to the side of the farmhouse. Shuffling the gift basket and her purse to her left side, she knocked on the front door.

After eight or ten knocks, and a few sore knuckles, Delanie wandered around back. She didn't see John's truck, but it could have been inside the barn. Opening the door to the screened-in porch, she made her way around piles of farm stuff, work boots, and an old wooden table with peeling paint. After no response to her knocks on the back door, she set the basket on the table and wrote on the card, "Thanks for a day at the Diamond! See you soon. Delanie."

On her way back to the Mustang, she stopped suddenly in the gravel driveway. She noticed small cameras under the eaves of the house and at the top of the barn, a lot of security for the middle of nowhere. Before she could ponder further, she heard a few barks. Within seconds, a pack of dogs surrounded her. They spanned the gamut from a miniature dachshund to a mottled Great Dane. Her panic at the pack of roving dogs evaporated when they all vied for her attention. One of the big dogs bumped into her and knocked her over, and the lickfest was on.

After pats and hugs and a lot of dog slobber, she finally managed to get back on her feet and to the car. She hoped that if John watched her escapades with the dogs from one of his many cameras that it wouldn't end up as a funny video on the Internet.

DELANIE ACCELERATED HER beloved Mustang to pass a large truck towing a camper on the Powhite Parkway. She told the car to dial Chaz's cell phone. After three rings, she heard an abrupt, "Speak."

"Hi, Chaz. This is Delanie Fitzgerald. Do you have a minute or two to answer a couple of questions?"

"Sure. What's up?"

"When we talked, you said that the homeowners association president Ken McDermott was trying to thwart your permits. How did you first come in contact with him?"

"When word got out that I was the new owner of the

property on Broad Street, I got a call from some board member of the association. He wanted to confirm that my plans for the property wouldn't clash with the design of the established neighborhood. Then he got nosey about what I planned to do to their fair community. I think he was sharpening the pitchforks."

"On what terms did the conversation end?"

"Probably not as well as it could have. When he got his panties in a bunch, I told him to mind his own business in so many words. Now that I think about it, some of them were probably very colorful words. I don't even remember the guy's name, but he got mad and I yelled. And then McDermott and his bunch declared war. It's been a shouting match ever since."

"Okay. Did you talk only by phone or did you all ever meet?"

"A couple of heated phone calls at first. They tried to schedule a meeting with me, but I told them to call my lawyer. After that, they took to the Internet. They've been defaming me for months all over social media. It's a good thing that most of my clients aren't big on reading online comments. It's really the principle of it, though. I'm not going to let them win with their whiney, tattletale tactics."

"Thanks so much for your time and information. I'll send you an update as soon as I do some more research. What's usually the best time to reach you?"

"I'm at the club a lot. I usually get there about two in the afternoon, and I leave about three in the morning. I like to take off on Sundays and Mondays. Try to avoid anything in the morning. I do my best work at night. You know, the cover of darkness and all that."

"Okay. I'll make sure not to call too early. Thank you again," said Delanie as she clicked off.

Glancing at the clock on the dashboard, she guessed that he was at the Treasure Chest now. That was good since the call was a ruse to find out Chaz's schedule.

She exited the expressway and followed the back roads to Broad Street and Chaz's house. She was pleasantly surprised when she got to the Church Hill neighborhood. Chaz had a condo in a neighborhood near Chimborazo Hill. Most of the older homes in the quaint neighborhood had been refurbished. Several newish condos looked like they had been dropped in among the classic townhomes from the turn of the last century. The tree-lined street offered a great view of the James River and the capital city.

Chaz's condo, one of the older ones, was third from the end with no cars in the driveway. Bursts of summer flowers in the beds on either side of the door buffered the house from the perfectly manicured postage stamp yard. She parked in the empty driveway and grabbed her clipboard to look official. Pulling a City of Richmond lanyard out of her purse with several laminated cards, she slipped it over her head. She hoped that no one would look at it too closely. A couple of the cards were backstage passes to recent concerts.

Climbing Chaz's three brick steps to the porch, she rang the bell and pretended to wait for a response in case anyone was watching. Enjoying the view, Delanie paused for what seemed like a reasonable amount of time. No one answered the door, so she moved on to the house to the right with a car in its driveway.

Delanie knocked on the neighbor's door. She heard a

shuffle and then the door opened a crack behind the storm door with bars.

"Yes?" a diminutive woman with tight white curls asked.

"Ma'am. I'm Courtney Owens, and I work for the city of Richmond. Your neighbor, Charles Smith, has applied to serve on the Community Relations Board, and I'm talking with some of his neighbors to see if he'll be a good fit."

"Oh, you mean Chaz next door? He's very quiet when he's here. Actually, he's not here much because he works a lot. He's always been a good neighbor, and he gives me the nicest Christmas presents. And he looks after my cats when I go to Cincinnati to see my sister."

"That's really nice. You're so lucky to have such a good neighbor. Would he be a worthy candidate to have on a community board for the city?" Delanie asked as she jotted fake notes on her clipboard.

"Well, I think so," she said. "He's always been polite and friendly. And he's a businessman, so I'm sure he could help you all out."

"Thank you so much for your time. Mrs. Uhhh?"

"Anderson. Mrs. Douglas Anderson, Jr."

"Thank you, Mrs. Anderson. What kind of business does Mr. Smith run?"

"He owns a restaurant downtown."

"Thank you so much. I appreciate the information and your time," Delanie said, smiling at Chaz's neighbor. Chaz must not drive his Hummer home.

Delanie turned and walked to the other neighbor's house. The driveway was empty, but she rang the bell and knocked because she could see Mrs. Anderson watching her from the front window.

When she didn't get a response to her knock, she walked back to Chaz's driveway. She was pleased with what she learned. Maybe old Charles Wellington Smith, III had another side. He seemed to have an alter ego that he used with his neighbors. Who would have guessed that Chaz was a cat sitter?

NINE

"I'LL BE RIGHT BACK," John Bailey said, pushing his straight-back chair away from the small table. It squeaked when it skidded across the tile floor at Olé, the Mexican restaurant on Belvidere Street.

When he was out of sight, Delanie grabbed his wine glass and wrapped it in a napkin. She stuffed it in her purse, hoping the napkin would soak up the last few drips of red wine. She pushed it down between her wallet and makeup bag to prevent it from clinking against her keys.

Delanie had called John earlier that week to see if he wanted to go to First Fridays Artwalk on Broad Street, a monthly street party that included some local art galleries and cafes.

Signaling the waiter to clear, Delanie checked her phone. Chaz had called twice and also sent a text. Ignoring his messages, she slid her phone next to the shrouded wineglass. John returned and pulled out his chair.

"You want dessert?" he asked, scooting his seat up to the table.

"No thanks, I'm fine. This was really fun and a great choice. I've never eaten here before."

John nodded toward the waiter and replied, "Yep, it was good. What do ya say we see what we can find on the artwalk?"

On the way to the first gallery, they passed a juggler and a guitar duo on the corner. Working their way through the crowd, they managed to get into Elise's Gallery, featuring black-and-white photography and a sculpture exhibit. Noticing Cooper Richardson with an entourage at the wine bar, Delanie moved closer. The mayor was nowhere in sight.

"Wanna drink?" John asked, interrupting her snooping. He touched her shoulder, and she jumped.

"Oh, no thanks. Wine with dinner was enough since I have to drive home. On second thought, maybe a ginger ale," she said, touching John's hand. She felt a tingle of electricity and hoped he felt it too. He was definitely difficult to read.

Waiting for John to return from the bar, she found an interesting life-size statue of a giraffe to admire while she spied on Cooper's party. After a few minutes of eavesdropping, she was disappointed that she didn't hear anything interesting from the mayor's aide except the group's plans for dinner and drinks tomorrow evening.

She and John perused the small gallery and then headed out to see what the next venue had to offer.

The next stop was the Switzer Gallery, full of performance art and mimes. Exiting after a couple of minutes, John put his hand on Delanie's shoulder and asked, "Are you ready for dessert now?" They walked past a fire juggler on a unicycle toward street vendors with carts of jewelry and snacks. The night air smelled like a mix of tiki torches and popcorn.

"No, thanks," she replied, stepping out on the street. "I've got to work tomorrow, so I better call it an evening soon. This was a lot of fun, and dinner was nice."

"Do you want me to follow you back to Chesterfield?" he asked, leaning closer.

Delanie caught her breath. He smelled like soap and Old Spice. She didn't want the night to end, but she needed to do a drive-by of Cooper's condo while she was downtown, even though she didn't expect the mayor's aide to be back anytime soon. Delanie didn't want to get caught stalking the mayor's assistant.

Talking herself out of staying with John, she said, "Oh, no thanks. I need to swing by my friend Ami's house before I head home. She lives on this side of town, and I have to pick up some documents from her. I had fun tonight. I hope we can do it again soon."

After they arrived at Delanie's car, he said, "I had a nice time. I'll call you." He then leaned in and kissed her. She was surprised at the sparks that turned into butterflies in her stomach. Delanie hadn't been interested in anyone in a long time. She took several deep breaths and then stepped into her Mustang. John waved when she drove off.

Her temples throbbing, she reminded herself that she still had work to do. A few minutes later, Delanie found on-street parking across from the condo at the Richmond Towers. She had to put John out of her mind for a while.

She had been staking out Cooper's residence over the last week in hopes of getting some information. So far, she hadn't recouped anything useful from all of her time there.

His building, a newish addition in the trendy part of town, sat between the Canal Walk and a restaurant in a refurbished factory. Walkways wended around what was left of other old buildings and an abandoned power station.

Delanie absolutely hated stakeouts. She tried to concentrate, but thoughts of John and their date kept interrupting her focus. This was the first time that she had ever bent the rules about getting too close to a subject. She hoped her relationship with John wouldn't sway her decisions about the job she had to do. But John was all that she could think about lately; he made her feel like she was sixteen again. All of the attention was exciting, and it would be over in an instant if she could prove he was Johnny Velvet. She could be kissing the eighties rocker whose poster had hung in her bedroom for years. That thought awakened the butterflies again and her pulse raced.

Delanie jerked forward in her seat in one of those moments where she wasn't sure if she had dozed off or not. Her subconscious kicked in, and she recognized the tall man with the shock of white hair entering the front door to the lobby. The illustrious mayor was easy to spot. The clock on her dashboard showed *12:42*. She stretched and tried to get comfortable in the car's front seat.

According to Duncan's research, Mayor Ed Hunter didn't live downtown. He resided in the old money neighborhood of Windsor Farms off Cary Street, where one of the homes was a Tudor estate that had been brought over, brick by brick, from England. It had been reassembled to give the new American owners a sense of English nobility on the banks of the James River. To Delanie, it looked like the mayor spent his other life in the trendy part of the city, far away from his old-money life with his respectable wife and his posh neighborhood.

Delanie stayed there waiting and watching until Cooper sashayed in about two-thirty in the morning. No one had left since the mayor entered the building. She called it an early morning and texted Duncan about an idea that she needed his help with.

DELANIE PULLED HER long red hair into a bun and stuffed it under one of her blond wigs that she kept for spying. She adjusted the wig and topped it off with one of Duncan's magic hats. The tiny camera, hidden behind the embroidered grizzly bear, would pick up the action. After she pressed the button, all she had to do was keep the bill pointed forward and her chin up.

She jumped out of the Mustang and parked around the corner from the Richmond Towers. Grabbing her clipboard and a potted plant with the baby blue bow that she bought at the all-night grocery store, she slammed the door and headed for the condo.

At this early hour, the front desk sat vacant. Her tennis shoes squeaked on the black marble floor. Delanie pushed the button for the fifth floor. This whole job was creepy, and she wouldn't relax until she was done with Chaz and his myriad of problems.

Duncan had uncovered the interesting fact that the tax assessment for Cooper's condo was recorded in the name of Edward G. Hunter. No spouse. He also found out that Mayor Hunter's grown son, Patrick, had listed the address as his last year.

Switching on the hidden camera, Delanie shuffled the plant to her left hand and knocked loudly on Coo-

HEATHER WEIDNER   75

per's door for what seemed like minutes. A barefooted Cooper finally opened the door. His appearance in jeans and a tan cashmere sweater with wet shower hair made him look so young. She hoped he didn't recognize her dressed-down blond look and put the pieces together that he had seen her previously on several occasions. Delanie looked beyond Cooper to see the mayor in the kitchen in a blue bathrobe and white socks.

Delanie panned the view by turning her head slowly for the benefit of the video recorder and said, "Hi, I have a delivery for a Mr. Cooper Richardson."

"Uh, thanks," he replied, taking the plant. Delanie turned and left before he could question the early morning delivery or offer a tip.

She slid in the Mustang's leather seat and let out a heavy sigh before she called Chaz and asked him to meet her for lunch. She had done a lot of spying on cheating spouses, but somehow, this case made her feel sleazy. She wanted to give Chaz the thumb drive and be done with him.

On the ride home, Delanie decided to make an extra copy for Ami, too. It might come in handy for the journalist's next article on the politics of the mayor's office.

TEN

THE GULLS SWOOPED and cawed overhead. Delanie used
the latest mystery that she had bought at the airport to
shield her eyes as she watched the birds' aerial acrobat-
ics. She sat on a bench across from the Bubba Gump
Shrimp Company on Navy Pier in downtown Chicago
and watched the birds in their frantic search for dis-
carded snacks.

Killing time while she waited for two o'clock, she
scanned the crowds. Depending on how the interview
went with Emily Jane Mercer, she was going to try to
catch a flight out of O'Hare for a return to Richmond.

Duncan had tracked down Johnny Velvet's daughter
and arranged the meeting at the end of her work shift.
Surprisingly, the young woman, who didn't have any
contact with her dad, was willing to talk to Delanie about
him.

The restaurant had a steady stream of patrons, and
Delanie wanted to get a table before Emily's shift ended.
The part-time waitress and full-time graduate art stu-
dent had agreed to a quick meeting.

The hostess seated Delanie outside near a wrought
iron fence. "Could you let Emily Mercer know I'm here?"
The hostess nodded and left a menu.

Delanie perused the one hundred-plus ways that one
could order shrimp. Her inventory was interrupted when

a tall blond with bobbed hair slid into the seat across from her.

Emily Mercer stuck out her hand. "Ms. Fitzgerald? I'm Emily Mercer. How can I help you?" Delanie secretly hoped that Emily Mercer would be nothing like her John Bailey.

"Thank you for agreeing to meet with me. As Duncan Reynolds told you, our firm has been hired by a writer in California to chase down some leads on Johnny Velvet sightings for her upcoming book. I appreciate your time. We're hoping you would be willing to do a cheek swab for us for DNA testing to put some of the rumors to rest," she said, shading her eyes with her hand. She wished she had brought her sunglasses.

"Uh, yeah, sure I guess," the younger woman said.

"No needles. You just open this kit and swab the inside of your mouth. We'll put it back in the envelope and send it away for testing. It's quick and painless."

"How long does it take?" she asked, popping it in her mouth and swishing it around.

"Best case, about eight-to-ten weeks at a private lab. But they have to do a lot of comparisons, so it could take months."

"Okay, here," she said, handing Delanie the kit. "I'd like to know the results because I never knew my dad. He and my mom split before I was born. My mom got a job here on WGN. Then, after my mom died, I moved in with my grandparents." Delanie stared at the young woman across from her.

The color and shape of Emily's deep blue eyes were identical to Johnny Velvet's, but that was about the only resemblance. She was the spitting image of her mom based on the photographs that Duncan had found on the Internet. Delanie wondered if her own subconscious was trying to rule out that John Bailey was Emily's father.

"Thanks," Delanie said, wrapping the sample and packing it in the bottom of her black purse. "Do you ever remember seeing your father?"

"No. He died before I was old enough to get to know him. My mom had some photos of him, but I never could find any of him with me. And I have no memories of him at all. When I was a teenager, I looked him up online. He looked like an interesting person. It's too bad that circumstances didn't work out for us before he died," she said, staring off at the crowds milling around near the Ferris wheel.

"Did your mom or grandparents mention anything about his life as John Bailey?"

"Uh, no. I do know that was his real name. But I don't remember anyone in the family ever talking about him except as Johnny Velvet. He and my mom weren't on good terms when they split, so we didn't talk about him much."

"The Vibes were one of my favorite bands growing up. I still like their music. Would you like something to eat?" Delanie asked, changing the subject.

"Oh, no, I ate on my break. Though I need to get going soon. I have to be at the studio this afternoon for my class. Would you like to order something?"

"No, thanks. I need to catch a flight back. I appreciate you taking the time to meet with me to talk about your father. And thank you for providing the sample."

"No problem, especially if it will put some of the ru-

mors to rest. It's no big deal. I get calls from reporters
from time to time when they do those where-are-they-
now shows on TV. This is the first time that I've had
anything worthwhile to contribute," she said, smiling.
She rose to leave.

"Thanks again." Delanie stood up and shook Emily's
hand. She watched the young woman turn and disappear
into the crowd. Delanie walked to the main entrance of
the pier in search of a cab to the airport.

Emily Mercer and their short conversation surprised
her. For someone who had faced that much sadness as
a child, she seemed pretty well adjusted. Delanie didn't
want to upset her world by uncovering that her dad had
been alive all this time a few states away. From what
little she knew about John, she couldn't see him aban-
doning his child.

John Bailey can't be Johnny Velvet and Emily's father.

GRABBING HER PURSE, Delanie walked from the con-
course across the breezeway to the parking deck at
Richmond International Airport. It had been a long day
in Chicago, and the flight had drained her. She longed
for Chinese takeout, a bubble bath, and bed.

She turned on her cell, and it immediately downloaded emails and buzzed with voicemail. The first was,
"Hey, girl! This is Ami. You're not going to believe
this, but it seems that Chaz has managed to get himself arrested. The idiot got charged with threatening the
mayor and attempted extortion. My source tells me that
he made bail. I'll call you later. Ciao."

Delanie clicked back to the timestamp. The call was
from ten that morning. Delanie wanted to get as far away

from Chaz as she could, but it was probably too late. It was just a matter of time before she received a call or visit from Richmond's finest, or her brother, about her unusual client.

Delanie texted Duncan a quick update about Chaz's latest escapades and then headed home for her date with takeout and the tub.

At home, Delanie grabbed the mail and placed Chinese food on the counter. She dropped her carry-on bag from the Chicago trip on the bed and drew a hot bath. Soaking in a bubble bath with a glass of shiraz and some dark chocolate was one of her guilty pleasures.

Pounding on the front door jolted her out of her relaxed state. Wrapping herself in a spa-sized towel, she threw on her fuzzy pink robe and slippers. She popped the rest of the chocolate in her mouth and left the wine glass on the counter as she moved toward the front of the house.

"I'm coming," she bellowed. Her announcement didn't help. The banging continued until she jerked open the front door, finding Chaz in mid-pummel on her storm door.

"What are you doing?"

"Sorry. I've got to talk to you, and you haven't been around," he said.

"How did you—" she stopped herself. It wouldn't have been hard for him to find her home address. "Come in." She looked over his shoulder to see what vehicle he had parked in her driveway. She let out a quick sigh, relieved that it was a black Mercedes instead of his bikini-decorated Hummer. Her neighbors were mostly retired folks, and his pimpmobile would have caused a stir.

Chaz burst in the door and paced like a tiger in a small cage around her tiny living room. Headlights from the end of the driveway shown in through the front window. Delanie looked out toward the yard, but it was just a dark colored truck turning around in her driveway.

"Please sit down," she said to the amped-up Chaz. "What is going on with you?"

"I can't sit down. I'm thinking about what to do next. I think the mayor has someone trailing me. I'm definitely being followed. And I think someone went through my trash this week."

"And now that person knows that I'm involved and where I live," she said, glaring at him.

"I didn't have anywhere else to go. The club is under constant police watch, and I needed to talk to you. You're the only one who understands my plight. And you didn't call me back."

Usually a fashion plate for the hipster generation, even though he had aged out of that demographic, Chaz looked out of sorts this evening in a wrinkled shirt, shiny suit jacket, and jeans. He continued to pace around the room, avoiding the front windows.

"When was the last time you slept?" she asked.

"I dunno. A couple of days ago, I think. My lawyer got me out on bail this morning. I spent the weekend in jail because of a vindictive district attorney who is a friend of the mayor. I took some stuff to get rid of a headache, and then it hurt worse. I had a few drinks before I got here to calm my nerves, but that didn't help either."

Delanie remembered her manners and softened slightly. "Are you hungry? I can split my Chinese takeout with you, or I could make sandwiches. There's also leftover pizza in the fridge." She wasn't sure what he had taken or how many drinks he had downed, but she figured that it couldn't hurt to get some food in him.

"Chinese sounds good," he said, following her to the bright yellow and orange kitchen. Delanie reheated the General Tso's chicken and divided it between two plates with the rice and vegetables.

"Do you have something to drink?" he asked.

She pointed to the fridge that he already had open. Chaz devoured his share of the dinner in seconds.

"Okay, what are your plans?" She situated herself on her end of the couch by the small TV tray.

"I dunno. I didn't rat you out to anybody. Actually, nobody asked where I got the information," he said, walking to the kitchen. She watched him rummage through her refrigerator.

"That's comforting. But what were you thinking?"

Returning to the living room, he said, "I wasn't. I was pissed about the permits and his holier-than-the-rest-of-you-peons attitude. I called up his office to complain for the tenth or twelfth time, and someone actually put me through to him. I guess my mouth took over before I could control it. But he deserved it."

"They arrested you for threatening the mayor and attempted extortion. Those are pretty serious charges," she said.

"It wasn't for money. I just wanted my permits to go through. I thought I could trade him the video for some assistance. Okay, in hindsight it probably wasn't a good idea." He finished off the leftover pizza that he had found in her fridge.

"Okay. What's done is done. I would recommend having no contact with him or anyone around him. You need to fly under the radar for a while. Do you think you can be quiet for a few days?"

"I know. I know. My lawyer read me the riot act. The mayor took out a restraining order against me," he said. His eyes darted around the room.

"Well, I appreciate your business, and I think Falcon Investigations has provided you with everything you asked for."

Chaz interrupted before she could finish her client brush off speech. "Sounds like you're dumping me."

"No, not really. I don't think you need the services of my firm anymore. You have the information you were looking for."

"Okay," he replied slowly. He was unusually silent for a few minutes.

"Did you need something else?" she asked.

"What else do you have around here to eat? I've got the munchies."

Delanie padded into the kitchen and replied, "I have a can of tomato soup, stuff for sandwiches, and some Pop Tarts."

"Soup and sandwiches would be good."

Delanie rolled her eyes and hoped that he couldn't hear her slam the pot and sandwich supplies around on the counter.

She served Chaz's next course, and he got up and returned with two more beers. It didn't surprise Delanie that neither was for her. She plopped down on the other end of the couch and surfed through the TV channels, hoping to land on something that didn't require too much thought. Chaz had worn her patience thin. And, she had lost count of all the beer he had consumed.

After slurping the soup and devouring the sandwich, Chaz cleared his throat and adjusted his place on the couch closer to her. He yawned and said, "I was hoping I could..." as all two hundred and some pounds fell on top of Delanie.

Outweighing her by at least eighty pounds, Chaz had Delanie pinned to the couch. She checked for a pulse and realized he was snoring softly. After several futile attempts to move him, she wriggled out of her robe and hurried to her room, grateful for the towel. Before she locked the bedroom door, she saw him slumped over on the couch on top of her pink robe.

ELEVEN

PULLING ON JEANS and a lightweight sweater, Delanie scooped her unruly hair into a ponytail. She slipped out of her bedroom to find her pink robe folded like it was on display at Victoria's Secret. It was propped up on the arm of the couch. No Chaz in sight.

Peeking out the front window, she saw Mrs. Obemeyer in her garden next door, but no Mercedes in the driveway.

In the kitchen, she found a note on the fridge.

Thanks, Delanie. I appreciate the hospitality. Call me if I can ever help you. You make the towel look good! Chaz.

Balling up his note, she tossed it in the recycle bin and curled her lip and hissed. Coffee and an onion bagel improved her mood.

Her cell phone buzzed with the Falcon Investigations ring tone. After a quick call between bites of bagel, she had a new case from her contact at Advance Insurance. She needed to check out a workman's comp case. It seemed that one Barry Cheeseman was so injured from lifting something heavy at his warehouse job that he could no longer work and needed to collect for his pain and suffering. Someone called in on a tip line that the terribly injured Mr. Cheeseman played in an adult volleyball league twice a week.

Delanie grabbed a change of clothes for volleyball tonight and headed to the office.

About twenty minutes later, she brewed a pot of coffee and settled in her office chair to go through her paperwork.

Deciding not to send John's wine glass or the napkin for testing, she wrapped them and put them in the Johnny Velvet box. She packaged Emily's sample for today's mail. Delanie assuaged the guilty feeling for not sending John's DNA. *I'll send it when I get a better sample than the glass,* she told herself.

Delanie spent the rest of the day reviewing and updating notes on John Bailey and Emily Mercer. It was odd that Duncan never showed up with Margaret.

Delanie's stomach rumbled. She looked at her watch and jumped up to change into a short black dress with spiked heels. She pulled her hair back and painted on the makeup. After a quick trip through the drive-thru for an early dinner, she ate out of a paper bag on her way to the volleyball club.

Parking in the half-full lot, Delanie found her way to the gym with three volleyball courts with two games already in progress. A handful of spectators dotted the stands. She checked her phone for a quick peek at Barry Chesseman's photo from the insurance agency. He sported an '80s retro look with jet black hair, cut short on the sides and longer in the back. *A mullet?*

There he was, front line on the middle court. It seemed that Mr. Cheeseman was a member of *Bust Your Balls*, and the team logo was hard to miss in dayglow orange.

For someone with a recent back injury, Barry was amazingly agile. He returned serves and slid down on his kneepads twice to keep the other team from scoring. Delanie recorded about twenty minutes of Cheeseman's athletic prowess before the game ended. She left the camera on and edged toward the first row where she found Barry rummaging through a gym bag.

When he looked up after finding his water bottle, Delanie hit him with her best smile and a flip of her ponytail. "Uh, excuse me. Do you know what team plays next?"

"No. But there's a schedule on that board over there. Who're ya looking for?" he asked, pointing across the court to the far wall and smiling at Delanie. He took a step closer to her.

"I was supposed to meet my sister Maggie here, but I don't see her. I guess I'll hang out for a while. Is your team finished playing?"

"Yup. What's your name?" he asked, smiling and stepping closer to Delanie.

"I'm Amber," she said, flipping her hair again for good measure. She thought Barry needed a lesson on personal space.

"Well, hello, redheaded Amber. I'm Barry Cheeseman, but my friends call me *The Cheese*." He pointed to his nickname in navy letters across his shoulders. "Some of us are going out for drinks. If your sister ditched you, you should join us. I'm sure you won't miss her too much. We're a friendly bunch."

"Thank you," she said with her best Southern accent. "But I think I better hang around here for a while. Maggie will be disappointed if I miss her game."

"Your choice. Here's my number if you change your mind," he said, writing his cell number on the back of a business card. "Hey, maybe I'll see you around. If you change your mind, call or text me."

She took his Pyramid Warehouse card and turned her purse to catch good footage of The Cheese. "Thanks. Appreciate it."

"Yup," he said, grabbing his towel and bag and following two women from his team to the back exit. He caught up to the women and joined their conversation.

Delanie waited long enough for him to leave the parking lot, and then she slipped out to submit her report about the athletic Mr. Cheese.

TWELVE

DELANIE CHECKED HER e-ticket for her connecting gate. It seemed like yesterday that she had traveled to Chicago, and now she had to fly from Richmond to Newark to finally get to Daytona Beach with all of the zigzagging flights.

Duncan had called yesterday with what he had pieced together from old news footage and clippings on who was at the Johnny Velvet accident scene. Jake "the Snake" Kowalski, the band's drummer, had survived the crash that killed Johnny Velvet, and Jake parlayed his fifteen minutes of fame into a second career. His brother, stuntman Kevin Kowalski, Kevin's girlfriend, and The Vibe's Manager, Bob Groome, were interviewed at the crash site. But it was not clear from the media accounts how they arrived at the scene so quickly after the accident, especially in the age before most had cell phones.

From Duncan's research, it appeared Jake was a regular at several of the bars in Daytona. According to sources, he would talk to anyone who would listen about the crash that killed his best friend. If Johnny Velvet faked his death, she wondered how Jake and all the other acquaintances had kept this big secret for so long. Delanie planned to look for any cracks in his story that she could exploit.

Jake and his brother's girlfriend were the only ones

still living who were at the accident site that fateful day. Jake's brother Kevin, a movie stuntman, died in his own fiery car crash on a movie set in 1998. And the group's manager died of a heart attack in a hotel room in Miami in 2003. The young blond with him at the time of his unfortunate demise wasn't Mrs. Groome. Duncan didn't know what happened to Kevin Kowalski's girlfriend—yet.

Delanie had some time to kill before her meeting with Jake later that evening at her hotel's restaurant. She had told him that she was a graduate student in American Studies doing an article on '80s bands, and he had seemed more than enthusiastic about helping her.

With just enough time before their rendezvous to check in and freshen up, Delanie took her stuff to the fourth floor of the Pirate's Cove. She didn't want to pay summer oceanfront rates, so her room overlooked the alley and the dumpster next door. She would rent a good hotel room if she ever took a real vacation.

Delanie put on the same outfit she wore for the Cheeseman job and then applied enough makeup for the glam rocker to feel right at home. She was pretty sure that the dress would work its magic on washed-up rock singers, too. She wondered what The Vibes drummer was like now. She grabbed her purse and double-checked that the door locked behind her.

The hostess seated her in an arc-shaped, leatherette booth in the back corner of the restaurant. If she looked over the wait station and three rows of tables, she could see the great Atlantic from the wall of windows behind the bar.

Delanie yawned and checked the time on her phone

for the fifth time. The Vibe's drummer was over forty minutes late. She was about ready to order without him when she spotted the aging rocker leaning on the hostess station. There was no way he could squeeze back into his leather pants from the heyday of The Vibes. The Daytona version was twenty-some years older and probably a hundred pounds heavier than the man on her poster. He used to have big blond hair, and now what was left was a sandy gray and shoulder length. His stringy hair ringed a puffy pink face.

The hostess brought him over to the booth, and he asked, "Caitlyn?"

"Yes, I'm Caitlyn Ross," Delanie said as she shook his outstretched hand.

"Well, hello. I'm Jake Kowalski."

"It's so nice to meet you, Mr. Kowalski," she said as he moved in close beside her in the huge booth. "Thank you so much for taking the time to tell me about The Vibes. I'm doing background research for my thesis, and it'll be such a big help. Do you mind if I tape the conversation? I don't know how I can thank you enough."

He snickered and replied, "Well, I'm sure we can both think of something later." He scooted even closer to Delanie.

Without missing a beat, he described every waking moment of life with The Vibes through drinks, dinner, and dessert. He only took breaks long enough to order another drink and go to the men's room.

During one of the breaks, Delanie asked, "Mr. Kowalski?"

"Please, call me Jake," he interrupted and grabbed her hand.

"Uh, Jake," she said. "Who was at the accident scene that terrible day?"

"Most of it's a blur." He was on his seventh drink and still going strong. She wondered if he blocked it out or whether his brain was so pickled he couldn't remember.

"Johnny and I had been at a cookout up in a fancy house in the Hills. We left about eight-thirty and were driving down toward the Mulholland Dam. It's at the base of the canyon with the hills in the background. You ever been to Hollywood?"

She shook her head, and he continued, "Well, you may have seen a picture of it. It's near the big Hollywood sign. Anyway, Johnny was driving over the bridge, and the car suddenly accelerated. I remember saying 'Oh, shit, we're gonna crash.' And then the next thing that I remember was waking up in an ambulance. By then, my brother and his girlfriend and our manager were there. They finally told me Johnny didn't make it. He and the car went over the side. They said I was ejected when it hit the bridge. We weren't wearing seatbelts."

He sniffed and continued. "I guess it wasn't my time, but I wonder every day why he died, and I didn't. I guess I haven't done what I'm supposed to do yet. There's not a day that goes by that I don't miss him. I also hope that I can honor his memory and keep it alive."

"I am so sorry for your loss, Mr. Kowalski," Delanie said, pulling her hands out of his grasp. But she stopped and patted the top of his hand for effect. "I have a few more questions if you don't mind," she said, looking through her notes.

He nodded, and she continued. "I've seen the video. Did they find his body when they pulled up his car?"

"Yeah. They did that later after we left. I think they had to get a crane."

"Where was Johnny Velvet buried? In Hollywood?"

"Uh, no, he wasn't," the aging rocker replied. "He was cremated. We sprinkled his ashes in the Pacific in a small, private ceremony. We didn't tell the press. We didn't tell anybody. Bob, Bob Groome, paid for a monument at that Westwood Cemetery. It's not a big graveyard, but a lot of musicians are there, and he thought that would be fitting. Johnny wasn't buried there, but they told all the fans that he was. Bob thought that the fans would need a place to visit. Johnny wouldn't have wanted a big scene at his funeral. It was ten or twelve of us on a pier at sunset. Then we went and drank to his memory at his favorite spot. Now that I think about it, the party may have lasted for a few days."

"Was Kelly Mercer there?"

"Who?" he slurred.

"Kelly Mercer. Johnny Velvet's girlfriend."

"Oh, no. She left with the kid long before the accident. She went back East somewhere, never to return. She wanted nothing to do with any of us."

"Did Johnny have any contact with his daughter?"

"I don't think so, but I don't remember. He was so excited when she was born. He talked about starting a family. But then we put out another album, which meant another tour, and the mother didn't want any more to do with rock 'n' roll. She couldn't go on the tour because of her job. She and the kid moved, and I think that was the end of it. I don't remember him ever talking about either one of them after they left for Chicago.

"Don't you think it's odd that he was happy about starting a family and then he never saw his daughter?"

"I dunno. The mother was a real piece of work. She was always giving him ultimatums, like get away from the LA lifestyle or never see his kid again. When that didn't work, she hinted the kid might not even be his. He was depressed for a while, but there were always girls around, so he wasn't lonely for too long. Plus, you don't miss what you don't have." When he finished speaking, he pointed to his drink and the waitress poured another refill.

"One more question, if you don't mind. What do you think about the folks who keep turning up, claiming to be Johnny Velvet?"

Wiping his eyes with the back of his hand. "Let's say we get a drink at the bar next door?" He paused and stared at Delanie. Finally, he resumed. "Liars, all liars. I was there that day. They want to cash in on the life of a great man. And it's just wrong," he said, signaling to the waitress for the check.

She put the tab on the table and refreshed his drink. Jake picked up the check. He quickly put it back down on the table. Delanie cleared her throat. "Thank you so much for all the information. Why don't you let me get that?"

He nodded, and she put her credit card in the folder face down and turned off her portable recorder.

"Shall we go?" he asked when the waitress returned with the receipt. Delanie scribbled a quick signature and closed the folder. They headed for the door, and Jake guided Delanie by her elbow to the nightclub next door.

Delanie wasted another two hours sitting on a barstool next to Jake. He told anyone who came near him about his past as drummer for a famous rock band in the '80s. He even posed for pictures with a few of them.

Around ten-thirty, when Jake turned his attention to two extremely thin blond women in cat suits, Delanie grabbed her purse and slipped back to her room. At least she left before she got stuck with another of his bar tabs.

Disappointed that Jake didn't reveal anything earth-shattering about Johnny Velvet, she was ready to head back to Richmond in the morning. Jake "the Snake" Kowalski talked a lot, but it was about his every waking moment with The Vibes. She kicked herself for not being more aggressive in her questioning. Maybe she should have surprised him with the theory that Johnny Velvet faked his death to gauge his reaction. Adding to her funk, John hadn't called. She only had three panicked voicemails from Chaz to listen to in her room.

THIRTEEN

TAKING A HUGE slurp of her iced chocolate, chocolate mocha with extra whipped cream and chocolate sprinkles, Delanie gave herself a brain freeze in the hot parking lot. She stood by her car for several minutes, holding her head. Hoping nobody thought it was a hangover, she locked the door and headed for the office.

"Hey, Dunc," she yelled from the empty lobby.

"In here," he replied. She stepped over Margaret, the bulldog, to find Duncan heating up his lunch in the tiny kitchen.

"How was sunny Florida?" he asked.

"Hot. Hotter than here," she replied, dropping her purse on the table.

"Good interview?" He turned to take his sandwich out of the microwave.

"Well, Jake Kowalski was talkative, but he didn't say anything that so much as hinted that Johnny Velvet faked his own death. Even drunk, Jake stuck to his story. He seems good at telling and retelling his tale with little variation. He did say they cremated him and sprinkled his ashes in a private ceremony. Then he said that the manager erected a headstone at a cemetery called Westwood. It was a place for fans to go and pay their respects. Should we even bother with the other around and listen." Duncan set up the call on speaker to be recorded. "Hopefully, I won't wake her up."

Delanie pulled up a guest chair to Duncan's desk. Margaret waddled in and took up residence on her puffy bed by the window.

After several rings, Duncan heard a fuzzy, "Hello?"

"Ms. Martinez, this is Duncan Reynolds with Falcon Investigations. Do you have a few minutes to talk? I was hoping you could help me with something."

"Are you the cops?" she slurred.

"No, Ms. Martinez. I'm a private investigator looking into the Johnny Velvet car accident. My research shows that you and Kevin Kowalski were close to The Vibes during that time. Would you mind answering a few questions?" he asked politely.

"I don't know what I could tell you that I haven't said over and over for the past twenty-some years. It's all pretty screwed up. First we lost Johnny, and then I lost Kevin. He was always pushing the envelope to make the stunts more exciting, and it finally killed him. He knew about the dangers, but he'd performed the stunt a bunch of times before. He knew how to blow up a car and make it fiery like it was real. But this time, the wind shifted, and he didn't leave himself enough time to get out. It's not fair. Things didn't turn out like any of us planned."

"I am so sorry for your losses," Duncan said. "Both of those car accidents were horrific. Did you stay in the stunt business?"

"Are you kidding? I'm not twenty-five any more. The jobs got farther and farther apart. There's not much call for a middle-aged stuntwoman. We weren't married, so there were no benefits or insurance for me. And not a day goes by that I don't miss Kevin and our life together. It just didn't turn out the right way. We had so many big plans," she sobbed into the phone.

"I am so sorry for your losses," Duncan repeated. "Could you tell us where Johnny Velvet is buried?"

"Uh, I don't know. It was some private affair. Kevin and I didn't go."

"Ms. Martinez, do you keep up with any of The Vibes?"

"Are you nuts?" she sniffed. "I don't work in the business anymore. I'm in retail now. It's a far cry from being a stunt double for all the Hollywood starlets. Johnny Velvet was lucky that he didn't have to deal with life after fame. He checked out while he was on top. What did you say your name was?"

"Duncan, Duncan Reynolds."

"Well, Duncan. You've ruined my day. I don't want to talk about it anymore. In fact, I don't want to talk to you anymore," she said, clicking off.

"Okay," Delanie said. "Life didn't go the way she wanted. Her comment about Johnny Velvet could be made to match our hypothesis. That's about the closest thing we've heard from any of his contemporaries who even hinted it was a set up. And she and Kevin were well versed in the art of fiery stunts."

"We have to keep chipping away at it. I'm looking into the other band members. And I'm gonna try the other end of John Bailey's life too. I've been able to track him in Virginia, but I can't find threads that lead back to anything in California for him as an adult. The name is very common, but everyone leaves some sort of paper trail. I usually don't hit a wall like this, but I'll keep at it. It's making me crazy."

"Thanks, Duncan. I know you'll find it if it's out there." Delanie scooted the chair back and returned to her office. She tried to muster the courage to call John. She hadn't heard from him in a while, and it was time to make something happen.

DELANIE SWALLOWED HARD to suppress the excitement that she hadn't felt since college. She pulled in and parked the Mustang next to John's farmhouse.

She climbed the steps to the large front porch and knocked on the door. A few minutes later, sporting a fresh-from-the-shower look, John answered the door.

"Come in. It's good to see you," he said, kissing her on the cheek.

"Thanks." She stepped into the living room that was once a parlor. The Victorian furniture and pink rosebud wallpaper had a frou-frou flair. His house didn't look like she imagined it. She was hoping for a man cave with clues to his '80s rock star status. It looked like John hadn't redecorated since his grandmother lived there.

Without asking her to sit, he guided her toward the front door and asked, "About ready to go?"

"Sure. Do you want to drive, or do you want me to?"

"I'll drive if it's okay. Your racecar looks too low to the ground. I'm used to my old truck. You know, slow and steady."

While John locked up, Delanie noticed a blue truck at the end of the driveway. It pulled in and backed out again by the time John had opened the passenger door for her.

"There aren't a lot of choices around here. Are you okay with Sergio's back in Chesterfield County?"

"That's fine. I order takeout from there from time to time. The food's good."

The ride back to her neck of the woods and dinner were fairly quiet besides pleasantries about what each had been doing lately. Delanie tried to sneak peeks every once in a while to see if John Bailey looked anything like Emily Jane Mercer.

It was almost eight-thirty when they made their way back to John's house. When they crossed the county line, John flipped on his headlights. The two-lane road wound between farmlands and wooded areas. Delanie watched for deer in the approaching darkness.

They rounded a bend, and a vehicle sped up behind them and rode John's bumper. The left lane was open, so it was odd that the person didn't pass. He tailgated John, and the headlights bore into the cab of the truck.

"Someone's in a hurry," John said, looking in his rearview mirror. He waved the other truck around.

The truck stayed on John's bumper for a few minutes. Then suddenly, the driver sped up and slammed into the back of the truck, just as the road curved. John's truck fishtailed, and he tried to get back in his lane. The dark-colored mystery truck sped off in the left lane. Delanie saw TREE on its license plate.

John yelled, "Shit! Hold on!" The truck bumped on and off the asphalt and slammed into a huge oak tree at the edge of the road. Delanie jolted, and the seatbelt jerked. The passenger side tires were in the soft shoulder, and the other two were on the pavement. The truck teetered and bounced, and then finally righted itself.

John shook his head. "Are you okay?"

"Damn. He came out of nowhere and then hurtled into you. I'm okay. But your lip's bleeding. And I think I'm going to have a bruise," she said, rubbing her shoulder. "The seatbelt kept me from flying around, but it dug in when we hit that tree." She wondered why the airbags didn't deploy, but then she realized the truck was too old to even have them.

"It's just a small cut," he said, wiping his face with his hand. "I think I bit it when we hit. That SOB came out of nowhere. He had plenty of room to pass, and there's nobody even out here. Dammit! Do you have your phone handy?"

Taking several deep breaths to calm down, Delanie finally replied, "Yep, I do." After several rings, she heard the state police dispatcher answer, and she gave her their location as best she could. There weren't too many landmarks in the country. *We're next to a bunch of trees wasn't that helpful.* She hoped that her voice didn't quake as she spoke to the dispatcher.

By the time the bleeding had stopped on John's lip, a state trooper pulled in behind them and turned on his blue lights that bounced around the dark woods. After the trooper took their statements, John started his truck and attempted to back up. He changed his mind when the passenger side bumper ground against the shoulder and the asphalt. When they couldn't get the passenger door open, John had the state trooper call for a tow truck.

After another hour of waiting, the tow truck driver hooked them up and was kind enough to drop them off at John's farm. Sitting on the porch swing, Delanie asked, "You sure you're okay?"

"Yep. Are you okay to drive? If not, you're welcome to stay over."

Delanie blushed. "I probably should be getting home, and I'm fine to drive. Could I bother you for a drink of water?"

"Anything stronger?"

"No, water's fine," she said. He wandered through the screen door to the kitchen.

Her private investigator side wanted to get inside the house to snoop, but she wasn't sure if she was ready for a sleepover. Before she could think any more about it, John returned with a cold bottle of water.

"Thanks. I had a good evening, despite the accident. Call me if you need a ride to get your truck."

"Okay. I had a nice time, too. Wish you didn't have to leave," he said, leaning in and lightly kissing her.

"I'll stay next time when you don't have a fat lip, and I'm not bruised. Call me this week and let me know how your truck is."

After a long hug, she headed back to Chesterfield before she changed her mind about staying.

Delanie oscillated between thinking about John and his invitation for her to stay and watching the road for the dark truck that never materialized. She didn't know if she was amped up from being extra vigilant or whether John had knocked her off kilter when he suggested that she spend the night.

FOURTEEN

DELANIE CLIMBED OUT of bed and winced. Bruises from the truck's old seatbelt radiated pain from her sternum across her chest and left shoulder. She stood and held onto the bedpost. Everything hurt more than when she went to bed. When some of the sharp pains subsided, she dragged herself to the bathroom. She hoped a warm shower would do the trick. It was probably a good idea that she hadn't spent the night at John's farm.

The pulsating water helped her muscles relax, but she had to be careful with deep breaths and plopping down on chairs. She gingerly put on jeans and a T-shirt and pulled her damp hair into a ponytail.

Grabbing a bagel and coffee, Delanie set up her laptop in the kitchen to catch up on clients' emails. Delanie did regular updates for all of her active clients, except Chaz. For someone supposedly trying to fly under the radar, he sent her lots of emails and texts. She hoped that he would get the message that she was ignoring him and fade out of her life. So far, it hadn't sunk in.

Her cell rang somewhere during her third cup of coffee and fourth aspirin. The butterflies jostled around in her stomach when she realized it was John.

"Hey, how're ya feeling?"

"A little sore. You?"

"I'm okay. The truck's not though. I'm coming your

way to look at new vehicles on the Motor Mile. Wanna get lunch?" he asked.

"That sounds nice."

"How about at Mexico on Hull Street at twelve-thirty?"

"Sounds good. See you then," she said.

Fighting the jitters, she changed clothes three times and shoes twice, despite the pain she felt each time she bent over.

Sliding into the red vinyl booth a few minutes before her date with John, she took a menu from the hostess and perused the lunch options. After two glasses of iced tea, Delanie spotted him in the restaurant's waiting area.

"Hi. Sorry to be so late. I planned to leave earlier, but Myrtle decided to bust out." He sat down across from her.

"Oh, hi," she said, getting lost in his deep blue eyes. "She okay?"

He nodded. "She gets obstinate from time to time. It took a couple of Twinkies to coax her back."

Lunch was just lunch with not much conversation. Disappointed, she reminded herself that it was a good thing that he wanted to see her, but the investigator in her was always looking for hints at hidden meaning. So far with John, there wasn't much innuendo.

John grabbed the check when the waiter set it on the edge of the table. "This has been nice, and I'm glad you could meet me. I'm heading down to look at new trucks. I haven't shopped for a vehicle in a while. Actually, it's been a really long time."

"Totaled?"

"Yep. It was old and not worth fixing. I was going to have it towed for a trade today, but I ended up selling it to the tow truck driver for a hundred bucks. I had to borrow a truck from the guy who helps me on the farm. I told the salesman I'd be by later this afternoon." He looked at his watch. "I'll miss my old truck. We've been friends for a long time. I guess it's time to update to something from this century... I better be getting on the road."

Delanie smiled and said, "I need to get going too. Thank you for lunch. I hope to see you again soon."

"We'll try dinner again, but without the road rage and the police. Here, use your magic on this." He handed her a scrap of paper with, "Blue Dodge Ram 2500 Laramie, TREEZ1" written on it. He kissed her on the cheek and said, "Bye," before she could ask any questions.

"Bye. Thanks," she said, hoping the surprise she felt wasn't showing on her face. She fingered the scrap of paper and wondered what he really knew about her. She had a hunch that he hadn't fallen for her freelance writer cover.

FIFTEEN

DELANIE'S CELL PHONE BUZZED, and she clicked the button on the steering wheel to answer.

"Hey, Dunc. What's up?" she asked, closing the car windows.

"Not much. I've been doing my homework, and I located the rest of The Vibes. Where are you?"

"I'm about ten minutes from the office."

"Okay, how 'bout if you grab lunch and meet me here, and we can pick which one to call first?"

"Sure. Any preferences for lunch?"

"Taco Bell. And get a soft taco, no lettuce, for Margaret."

"Will do." She clicked off and merged right to swing into the shopping center for the fast food.

Delanie settled into her desk chair with her tacos and a blue soft drink. Duncan sat across from her, where Margaret mauled what was left of her taco on the carpet in the hallway.

Wiping his mouth on the back of his hand, Duncan started. "Okay, you've met Jake Kowalski, and we didn't get much out of your Daytona trip except that he's making the most of his presence at Johnny Velvet's accident scene as his way of getting free drinks and impressing younger women. And conversations with Jake Kowalski's brother's girlfriend didn't yield much either. I have contact info for the other three members. Where should we start? Will Lane is a music producer in Los Angeles. David Moore is a drive-time DJ at a Top 40 station in Philadelphia, and Eric Davis teaches music in Austin, Texas. They all do something sort of musical, but nothing close to being a member of a popular rock band during the big '80s. I wonder what Davis tells his students about his past life?"

Delanie shrugged and handed him a napkin. "Dunno. But it's the middle of the day. Who's likely to answer the phone?"

"Davis teaches in a middle school. We probably can't reach him until later this afternoon, even with the time difference. Let's try Moore. He does some sort of morning show. So maybe we'll get lucky," he said, punching in a long distance number. "Plus, he's on the East Coast."

After three rings, a gruff "Hello" came through the speakerphone on Delanie's desk.

"Mr. Moore, this is Delanie Fitzgerald from Falcon Investigations. Do you have a few minutes to talk with my partner and me?"

"Whatcha need?" he asked.

"We're private investigators from Richmond, Virginia, and we want to ask you a few questions about Johnny Velvet and The Vibes."

"That was a lifetime ago," he replied in a muffled voice.

"Mr. Moore, this is Duncan Reynolds. Could you tell us where you were the day of the accident?"

"I was in Vegas with my first wife. We had some time off between the recording studio and touring. I heard about it from Bob. He called and left a message for us at the hotel."

"Bob Groome, your manager?" Duncan asked.

"Yep," replied the aging rocker, clearing his throat.

"Did the rest of you talk about carrying on the band after the funeral and all the media hype calmed down?" Delanie wasn't sure what Duncan was driving at, so she remained quiet.

"No, not really. It was a rough time for all of us. We had been on top for three years. By then, the cracks were starting to show. Will was making noises about going solo, and Johnny was pretty much over all the crap that comes with the business side of music. We were barely speaking to each other by the time of Johnny's death. I'm not sure how much longer The Vibes would have lasted even if the accident hadn't happened." After a long pause, Moore continued. "Eric and I loved being part of that band. It was the life that we dreamed about as kids. After the accident, nobody wanted to continue on as it was. I mean, how could we without Johnny? He created The Vibes. He was our leader. We hung out for a while, but we eventually drifted off to other projects. Last I heard, we were scattered all across the country."

"Did you come back from Vegas for the funeral?" Duncan asked, fidgeting in Delanie's office guest chair. Margaret waddled in and settled at Duncan's feet. She licked her paws and stretched in preparation for her next nap.

"Oh, yeah. Me and Cassidy, my first wife, rented a car and drove back to Los Angeles the first thing the next morning. There was a lot of media buzz and interviews. We stayed in town until a couple of days after the funeral. It was a crazy, sad time. A lot of it's a blur to me now."

"One last thing. Where was he buried?"

"Uh, Hollywood in that big cemetery, I think the name was something like Hollywood Memorial Gardens or Hollywood Gardens. Girls camped outside the gates for days. It was insane. We did so many TV interviews. It was a whirlwind. We were on MTV constantly. And then it was over as quickly as it started. The TV cameras were whisked away to the next hot story, and we all eventually moved on... I miss him. Not a week goes by that I don't think about Johnny. We had an incredible romp as The Vibes. It was more than any of us could have ever imagined. Wow. Lots of great stories."

"Mr. Moore, do you have regular contact with the rest of The Vibes?" Delanie asked.

"Nah, not too much anymore. We did a couple of those 'where are they now' nostalgia shows for VH-1, and I get a call every few years, usually around the anniversary of the accident from some reporter who wants a comment. Last I heard, Will's still in LA, and Eric's a schoolteacher in Texas. Will and I stayed in the business. But Eric got out and didn't look back. And who knows where Jake ended up. Is he even still alive?"

"Yes," Delanie replied. "He's living in Daytona Beach."

"That's good. I'm glad he's still kickin' around."

"Mr. Moore, did Johnny Velvet do everything under his stage name?" Duncan asked. "I mean, did he sign contracts, checks, and stuff under Johnny Velvet, or John Bailey?"

After a long pause, the rocker-turned-DJ said, "Uh, I think he did everything as Johnny Velvet. I never remember anyone ever referring to his real name. Now that you mention it, I don't think I ever remember him signing anything except contracts. And yep, he always signed Johnny Velvet. I'm pretty sure of it. He was always Johnny Velvet when we were The Vibes. He never talked about his life before the band."

"How did you all meet?" Delanie asked.

"In college. Will, Eric, and I were roommates. Jake was Johnny's roommate. Will knew Jake. We played some gigs in LA and got lucky when Bob heard us at the Roxy. We got a record contract, and that was the end of school."

"Were you all based in LA then?" Delanie asked.

"Uh, yeah. We had an apartment together to keep down the cost of living expenses. Will and I stayed there mostly, but the others always seemed to be around."

"Did Johnny Velvet have family nearby then?"

"I dunno. If he did, we never met them. He brought a few girlfriends by to meet the band, but I don't remember ever meeting any of his family."

"Can you tell us anything about the accident or the investigation?" she asked.

"Uh, no, not really," he replied. "We were in Vegas when it happened. I don't remember anybody talking about an investigation. It was the Decade of Excess. Everything, including a funeral, spawned a party."

"Well, thank you very much for your time, Mr. Moore. We appreciate all your help and the information."

"Sure," he said, clicking off without waiting for any other questions.

"Hmm. I guess he still considers himself as being in the business," Duncan said.

"Maybe, like Jake, he's not ready to give up being a performer. I guess it's a long way down when you have to get a job and start living like the rest of us."

"I looked through the station's website and promo material. They play Top 40, but Dave Moore has a show called the 'Big Eighties,' and he does public appearances in the metro Philadelphia area. Like Jake, he's still living off his Vibes success. It sounds like Eric Davis was the only one to get out. If he can live a normal life as a teacher in Texas, it stands to reason that Johnny Velvet could pretend to be dead and live as John Bailey in rural Virginia," Duncan said, clicking the keys on his laptop.

"I guess. But I'm not totally convinced that John Bailey is Johnny Velvet. Some of the timelines work, but other things don't quite match up."

"Do you want to call the other guys in the band?"

"Not now. We're not getting much from them," she said.

"Hey, look at this. On the Hollywood Memorial Gardens' site in California, there's no mention of Johnny Velvet in their list of notable inhabitants. They have a flashy website with a map to all of the famous graves. It looks like a tourist attraction. There is no Johnny V. listed anywhere. I'll call and verify, but it doesn't look like Johnny Velvet is buried where David Moore said he was. Hey, hmmm."

"What?"

"There's this little tiny article that I missed the first time. There is a monument for Johnny V. at the Pierce Brothers' Westwood Village Memorial Park."

"That's what Jake said."

"It's still fishy that two bandmates gave us different final resting places for Mr. Velvet. One said he was buried, and the other said he was cremated. Maybe it was all hazy from the sex, drugs, and rock 'n' roll. But both stories were told without any hesitation. Sasha Martinez's story was close to Jake Kowalski's explanation. What do you think about this idea? Maybe some of the players weren't in on the hoax, and they think Johnny is really dead. That might make it easier for the secret to stay buried so long."

"Funerals for famous people, even fake funerals, usually generate some kind of publicity," Duncan said. "I'll do some more checking, but there are too many holes in this story for my taste. I couldn't find any footage or stills of the funeral. MTV showed quite a few spots about the accident, but nothing at the cemetery. I'll call and see when Bob purchased the monument. It's a little strange that there are some big holes in their versions about the end of Johnny Velvet. It's all a bit suspicious."

"You're right. There're a lot of pieces missing in this puzzle. I'm heading out in a few. Do you need me to do anything tonight?" Delanie started cleaning up.

"What, a quiet night at home? Nobody to stalk?"

"Nah," she said, pulling her sunglasses and keys out

of her purse. "I don't get to be Nancy Drew every night. Sometimes it's just me, ice cream, and the TV."

Duncan looked like he was about to say something, but she left the office before he could.

SIXTEEN

DELANIE ROLLED OVER and looked at her cell phone vibrating across her nightstand at four-fifteen in the morning.

"Uh, hello."

"Delanie, it's me," slurred the speaker.

"Who?" she snapped.

"Chaz. Sorry to bother you so early, but we've got a problem, a huge problem."

"What are you talking about?" she asked.

"Tonight after closing. It's not good. This is really terrible. Just terrible." He sniffed.

"Are you okay? I can hardly hear you."

"No, I'm not okay, and I don't know what to do. This is so bad. Marco went out a couple of hours ago about closing time. There was a car in the fire lane out front with a guy slumped over. Dead. With lots and lots of blood," he whispered.

"You know who it is?"

"Delanie, you've got to listen to me. It's the mayor! He's dead in a car in front of my business."

"What?" Delanie shrieked. She bolted upright and turned on the light.

"The mayor. Marco found him dead outside my club. The place is crawling with cops."

"Are you still downtown?" she asked, pushing a clump of curls away from her forehead.

"Yep. The police have been in and out over the past few hours. Most of the street is blocked." His voice trailed off.

"Uh, can you get out to meet me somewhere?" She rubbed her eyes and tried to focus on Chaz's dilemma.

"Nope. My car's in the lot that's blocked by the police. But we have a back door. You could get in, park, and walk up on 18th Street. Marco'll let you in."

"Okay, okay. I'll call you when I'm close to your place," she said, sliding her legs over the side of the bed.

"Thanks, Delanie. I left a message for my attorney, but he's out of town. Bye." He clicked off before she could change her mind.

Delanie showered in record time. She slipped on black jeans and a plain T-shirt. Pulling her wild hair up in a ponytail, she slapped on a touch of makeup and then grabbed her keys and purse.

After a stop for coffee and a bagel at the all-night gas station and texts to Duncan and Ami, Delanie sped her way through the tollbooths toward downtown.

Parking on the street about two blocks away, she made her way to the Treasure Chest, zigzagging through a warren of one-way streets and alleys in the Shockoe Bottom neighborhood. Surprised at the lack of police presence at the back entrance, Delanie called Chaz.

A few minutes later, a man in black leather opened the gray industrial door with no windows.

"Come in." Marco, the bald bouncer, filled the whole doorframe.

When he stepped back, Delanie followed him into a dimly lit room. He shut the door hard and slid the bolts into place. She trailed him down the back hallway through the kitchen and food prep areas. Passing storage rooms and bathrooms, Marco led her to Chaz's office, which was less offensive than Delanie had imagined. She had visions of early brothel with a lot of red, fuzzy wallpaper. She spotted Chaz sitting behind a black lacquered desk. He looked older today than she remembered, and his hair hung limply around his face.

Chaz pointed to the empty guest chair while Marco remained standing in the doorway.

"This just can't get any worse. I don't know what I'm gonna do."

"Okay. What exactly happened?"

"Tell her, Marco," Chaz said, looking up at the mountain of a man who looked like a cross between a linebacker and a biker.

Marco made no move to sit. After a long silence, he said, "About one-thirty, I went out front after one of our bouncers said someone parked in the fire lane. I approached the black Mercedes. There was an old white dude slumped across the front seat. I got no response when I tapped on the glass and yelled at him."

"Did you open the door?" Delanie asked, craning her neck to see Marco's face.

"I thought it was a drunk passed out over the steering wheel. I opened the door, and when he didn't move, I pushed him back against the seat. I went to take his pulse, but after seeing the front of his shirt, I knew I didn't have to worry about a heartbeat or nothin' else. I thought he was just another drunk."

"So, then what?" Delanie asked.

"I called 911, and the Richmond PD sent a car by. The cop knocked on the window, and of course, he didn't get any response either. It was definitely a gunshot. Somebody made some big holes in the mayor's chest," Marco said, pulling out his phone. He thumbed through pictures.

"Can you send me those?" Delanie asked.

He nodded and handed her his phone. She tapped in her contact information into Marco's phone.

Delanie let out a sigh and sank back into the fake leather chair. She flipped through Marco's pictures on her phone when they downloaded. It was obvious that the corpse was the mayor.

"When do you expect to hear back from your attorney?" Delanie asked, looking at Chaz. He shook his head. "You probably should call his office and ask his assistant to get in touch with him wherever he is. You're gonna get a lot more attention soon, and it's not the good kind."

"This has already gotten a lot of attention." Chaz covered his head with his arms.

"You're in for a lot more. This is just going to get uglier and uglier."

Chaz nodded and turned to rifle through a drawer. "Delanie, I know you've done all that I've asked, but I need one more favor." She sighed again, and he slid an envelope toward her. "I swear I didn't kill him. I was here all night, but I don't know if that's gonna matter. I need you to find out who murdered him. If this amount isn't enough, let me or Rick, my lawyer, know. You've got to find out who set me up."

"Chaz—"

He interrupted. "Delanie. I need you to do this for me.

I know from your past work that I can depend on you. I didn't like the mayor, but I wouldn't kill him."

"Okay, okay," she said. "Against my better judgment, my firm will look into it. Do you have video from your security cameras? Anything facing the front of the building?"

"Yep. The police swooped through here and took a bunch of stuff including footage from the surveillance cameras; Jimbo always makes copies of everything. One of my guys is back there looking through what we got right now. Marco'll show you down there to see what security found so far."

Delanie followed Marco down another long hallway through a bar area, decked out in early pirate. Kitschy, but not what Delanie had imagined. Without all the flashing lights, it resembled a dance studio where each vertical pole had a crow's nest at the top. For a fleeting moment, Delanie wondered what it would be like to be on one of the elevated stages. Then she thought about what went on here and in the back rooms. She shuddered and wondered if she had any hand sanitizer in her purse.

After a trip down another dark hallway, Marco led her to a small closet with a bank of video monitors and two ancient office chairs.

"Jimbo, this is Delanie. She's Chaz's PI. Anything?" Marco asked.

"Nah, you can see the car pull in from the side street." Jimbo crushed a cigarette in a soft drink can. "You can't see who was driving or if anything happened on the street."

"Keep looking," Delanie said. "Sometimes, you catch

something where you don't expect to. Can you slow it down a bit at the point when the car rolls into the frame?"

Jimbo nodded and Delanie sat down next to him. She scooted her folding chair closer to the small monitors.

She never imagined that she would be spending this much time in a strip club, and she sure wasn't going to tell her brothers.

SEVENTEEN

AFTER FOUR HOURS of reviewing grainy surveillance video, Delanie rose from the office chair that probably dated back to the Reagan years and winced. *Still sore*, she thought. She rubbed her tired eyes and asked, "Anything to eat around here? Snack machines or coffee?"

"Yep, there's a kitchen in the back. Sandwich okay?" Jimbo asked.

"The kitchen's open?"

"Yep, crew is probably stocking or prepping something. I guess we'll open tonight."

"A sandwich would be good. You watch these cameras all the time?"

"Almost every night," Jimbo said as he called someone to ask for sandwiches and coffee. Hanging up the phone, he said, "Me and my crew sit in here seven nights a week and watch everything on those little screens."

"It must be an interesting job."

"Not really. You get numb to it after a while. You're always looking for what's out of place, so everything else becomes background noise."

After good ham sandwiches and strong, black coffee, Delanie decided to wrap it up. They couldn't find anything useful from any of the camera angles that monitored the entrances and the parking lot.

"Well. Thanks for letting me hang around. Tell Chaz I'm going back to the office to look into some things."

Jimbo nodded and returned to his bank of black and white monitors and the video feeds.

Delanie stepped out into the hall and ran into Marco.

"Oh, sorry. I was just heading back to my office," she said, stepping back in order to see Marco's face.

"Where are you parked?"

"A couple of blocks over."

"I'll go with ya because it's still a circus out there," he said as he turned toward the club's rear exit.

They walked in silence to her car. When they approached her parking spot, Delanie pointed to the black Mustang.

She jumped when Marco put his massive hand on her shoulder. "Chaz was in the club all night, I swear."

"Okay, I'll see what we can find out. It's going to get worse before it gets better, and he's in a lot of crosshairs right now. Make sure he remembers to call his attorney. Hop in, and I'll take you back."

"Nah, that's okay," he said. "I won't fit in your sports car. See ya around." The bouncer disappeared down a side street before she could start the car.

Delanie looped around the corner to see how close she could get to the front of the club. The authorities had blocked off close to a three-street perimeter, and news crews took over where the police cars stopped. Trucks from outside of the Richmond area were setting up camp outside the police tape. Behind the last remote truck, Delanie spotted the big truck with the TREEZ plates, but there wasn't anyone inside. Delanie made a quick turn down a side street and headed for the office.

The blue truck sightings were happening too often to be a coincidence. She had to find out if Duncan had traced the license plate.

Parking in her normal spot next to Duncan's canary yellow Camaro, Delanie checked the mail and let herself in the office.

"That you?" he yelled from the back.

"Yep. I've been hanging out at the Treasure Chest all morning." She stood in the doorway of the conference room, watching Duncan adjust the sound on the flat screen. He had rigged it to show three local newsfeeds on one screen. Two were doing minute-by-minute updates on Mayor Ed Hunter, "Crisis in the Capital City." The ABC affiliate had returned to normal programming with a red crawl across the bottom of the screen.

"So, you've been hanging with the T & A King again. The company you keep, Delanie," he said, shaking his head.

"More like hanging with his minions. I've looked at hours of video feed from every possible angle. The police took the video surveillance, but Chaz's guy had copies."

"Anything good?" he asked, looking up from his laptop.

"This." She tossed Chaz's envelope with eight thousand dollars on the table. "Other than that, no. Just hours and hours of cars coming and going. They had one shot of the car pulling in. We got a timestamp of 1:18 AM, but you couldn't see the driver or anyone else. Chaz may be a sleaze, but at least he pays in cash and on time."

"Too bad there was no useable video. Wonder if the

cops got anything from the businesses across the street from Chaz's club," Duncan said.

She shrugged and dropped the mail on her desk in the next office and returned with her laptop. "I dunno. I didn't go door to door. Most of the nearby establishments are nightclubs, and they didn't look like they were open. I spent time with Jimbo, the security guy, and Marco, the head bouncer. Marco alibied Chaz, but I still think it's a matter of time before Richmond's finest come for him. The club was still surrounded by cops and television news crews when I left."

"I've been watching the local footage. The town's going to be in mourning for the next few weeks. The family hasn't made a statement yet, but they keep interviewing average Richmonders, and they're outraged at how something like this could happen in our fair city. By the time this is over, I'm sure they'll have interviewed everybody who had ever spoken to the mayor. They're definitely not painting a travel brochure depiction of Chaz's part of town. A bunch of the folks interviewed want to close down the Treasure Chest. I wouldn't be surprised if the torches and pitchforks come out soon. Chaz is definitely not popular right now. If he doesn't get arrested, he might want to lay low for a while."

Duncan turned the sound down when one of the young blond reporters noted that the mayor's married daughter, Melissa, and her husband, the congressman, were cutting short their trade junket to Japan to return home to be with the family.

To get her mind off of Chaz and his problems, Delanie spent part of the afternoon drafting a report on the

Johnny Velvet investigation. She had procrastinated way too long on this. John Bailey threw her off-kilter. This was new territory, and she was afraid that she might have gone too far. She usually didn't care how an investigation unfolded, but this was different.

She was picky about men, and John Bailey was ruggedly handsome and sweet. But he didn't have enough *wow* qualities to hold her attention for long. Yet, there was some sort of thrill in the possibility that he might be the rocker she adored as a girl.

EIGHTEEN

DELANIE NEEDED A break from her investigations of John Bailey and Chaz Smith. She found a brief solace at her friend Paisley Ford's salon.

While lying back in the shampoo chair, Delanie heard her cell beep from inside her purse. Paisley turned from the shampoo bowl and said, "I'll hold the towel. Go ahead and answer it."

"Thanks," Delanie whispered, grabbing the purse and fishing out the phone.

Paisley bunched up Delanie's hair in a towel, and Delanie stood and duck walked while she balanced the phone.

Duncan's number flashed on her screen. She pressed the button and heard, "Delanie, Richmond PD arrested Chaz this morning."

She let out a heavy sigh. "We kinda knew it was coming, but this isn't good. Thanks for the update. I'm not sure when I'll be back in the office."

"I'll call you if I hear anything else. See ya."

Delanie returned to her chair, and Paisley applied conditioner and started snipping the split ends.

"That was Duncan. My best-paying client managed to get himself arrested again this morning."

"It didn't sound like it was a surprise." Paisley shook

her head as she talked, and her blond curls bounced and returned immediately to their perfect position.

"My client's been under police surveillance for a while. Down deep, I don't think he did it. I just have to figure out a way to prove his innocence. Things are going to get bad for him."

"Delanie Fitzgerald, sleuth extraordinaire. Go get 'em, girl! Figure out who killed the mayor."

"Hopefully, it'll work out for my client. He's not even close to being a model citizen, but he kind of grows on you after a while. Thanks again for taking me early."

"Not a problem. It's the quiet part of my day, and it gives us a chance to catch up. We need a girls' night out. When can you do something?"

"Dinner next week?"

"Hmmmm. I'm leaving Thursday for a couple of days with Kyle. We're going to his family's beach house near Jockey's Ridge in the Outer Banks."

"Kyle? Stephen was the love of your life the last time we talked." She hoped Paisley didn't hear her sigh.

"Didn't work out. Stephen was a mama's boy who needed her input and approval on everything. It was really crowded in that relationship. Kyle is fun and smart, and if it doesn't work it's probably because he's kind of young."

"How young?" Delanie sat up and examined her friend's work in the mirrors as Paisley continued snipping.

"Almost twelve years younger. But you can't say a word because I don't think he's figured it out yet."

"Sounds like you're a cougar. When are you going to tell him?"

"When it becomes an issue, so maybe never. You just can't come to any more of my birthday parties unless you swear you were my babysitter."

"Oh, yeah right. You know your friends won't keep that secret."

"Then maybe I won't let him meet anybody for a while," Paisley said, staring off into space.

Delanie checked the back of her head in the mirror. "Looks good. Thanks."

"You're welcome. Kyle is really wonderful. He works in investments at one of the big firms downtown. In his spare time, he hikes, runs, and kayaks. We're going to have so much fun at the beach," she said, spinning Delanie around to face the door.

"You? With Mr. Outdoor Sporty Spice?"

Delanie's thoughts drifted to Chaz and his host of problems as Paisley scrunched Delanie's curls in the diffuser. The guys at the club had alibied him, but the police had arrested him anyway. Someone must have thought there was enough evidence to move forward.

"Tah-dah!" Paisley spun Delanie around to see all sides of the triple mirrors.

"Looks good as usual. How much do I owe you?" Delanie asked, fingering her soft curls.

"Don't worry about it. You just pick up the dinner and bar tab for our next adventure."

"Deal." Delanie hugged Paisley, who folded the black and white dotted smock. "Have fun this weekend, and good luck with the boy toy."

The bells on the front door tinkled when Delanie exited. Grabbing her sunglasses, she waited for the Bluetooth in the Mustang to connect to her phone. Turning out of the strip mall, she decided to go downtown to do a drive-by of Cooper Richardson's condo.

When the phone connected, she dialed information and asked for the mayor's office. The automated voice found the number and connected her.

After five rings, Delanie heard, "City of Richmond, Office of the Mayor. How may I direct your call?"

"Cooper Richardson, please."

"One moment," replied the soft Southern voice who didn't wait for a response before she clicked off.

"Mayor's office," said the next voice.

"I'm trying to reach Cooper Richardson." Delanie checked the traffic in the rearview mirror and changed lanes.

"I'm sorry. Mr. Richardson is not in today. Would you like his voicemail?"

"Do you know if he'll be in tomorrow?" she asked. She passed a truck to get in the E-Z Pass toll lane.

"I don't have his schedule yet. Would you like his voicemail?" repeated the clipped voice with the New York accent.

"Yes, thank you." Delanie listened to Cooper's stock message, but it didn't give a clue about when he was coming back. She hung up before the beep.

Delanie exited the Downtown Expressway and navigated the back streets until she reached what was left of the historic Haxall Canal. Cooper's fancy condo overlooked the James River with the canal on one side and the Federal Reserve Bank on the other. She parked and strode into the lobby of Cooper's building. Today, a guard in a security uniform sat behind the semicircle desk.

Delanie cleared her throat. "Excuse me, could you

call up to Mr. Cooper Richardson's condo and let him know that I'm here. I'm Jocelyn Jones. He should be expecting me." She flipped her curls over one shoulder.

The guard with the military flat top cut straightened up to attention in his seat. "Mr. Richardson left early this morning. Do you want me to leave him a message?"

"Oh, pooh!" Delanie said, stomping her foot on the black marble floor. "He did say to meet him here this Saturday. It was the only day he had available this week," she said with her best pouty bottom lip.

"But it's Friday."

"Friday? Oh, phooey! I can't believe I mixed up the days. Please don't tell him I was here, or he'll think I'm a total goof," she said as she did her best to give a sheepish, ditzy look. "I'll be back tomorrow," she said, fluttering her eyelashes.

"No problem. I'd say see ya tomorrow, but I'm not here on Saturdays."

"Well, maybe we'll run into each other some other time." She waved to the guard as she headed for the door.

Delanie had one more place to check, but it would have to wait until this evening. This was the third drive-by this week with no results, and she'd had no luck with his home or work numbers either.

Something was bothering her, but she couldn't pin-point what was tugging at the back of her brain. She needed to talk to Cooper again, but it had to look like an accidental meeting.

NINETEEN

It was a big night out in the Fan district. Not finding any on-street parking near Freeda's nightclub, Delanie circled the block several times until she found a spot in the tiny lot behind the bar. After hiking around the building in her stilettos, she smoothed her purple dress and fluffed her hair with her fingers before entering the club.

No one was in the lobby. She made her way to an empty stool at the end of the bar and ordered a white wine. Everyone else was in small groups or with a partner. The place looked bigger with no one on the dance floor. Sipping her drink, Delanie checked out the occupants. One of the Nordic-looking bartenders was on duty. He didn't act like he recognized her when she ordered. She didn't see Deke and had no idea about his work schedule.

Delanie spotted a disheveled Cooper Richardson at a table near the restrooms. Sitting alone with several empty glasses, he was unshaven, and his clothes looked like his cat had slept on them for two days. She waved over the bartender.

"Excuse me. Could I get another drink? Whatever he's having," she said, pointing to Cooper, whose head was in his hands.

"Sure," he replied. A minute later, he placed a whiskey sour on the bar. Delanie paid and over-tipped him.

Sliding off the barstool, she moved over to the small table next to the hallway and the restrooms.

"Excuse me, Mr. Richardson, I thought you'd like a refill."

"Huh," he said, looking up. He had aged ten years since she had seen him last.

"I'm Meagan Martin. We met a few weeks ago at the Flying Squirrels game."

He nodded politely without the look of any recognition. Pressing the heels of his palms into his face, he rubbed his eyes.

"Well, anyway. I didn't want to bother you. I just wanted to offer my condolences on the death of Mayor Hunter. It was so tragic and sudden."

"We're never prepared," he said. "Please sit down if you'd like. I'm sorry, I'm not at my best. Refresh my memory here. Where do I know you from?" His bloodshot eyes were ringed in red, and his face was puffy.

"Oh, I'm terribly sorry," Delanie cooed. She sat down across from him. "I'm Meagan Martin. I work with Joe Smith and Tom Taylor in catering. We were with the food vendors when you all came through the Squirrels game last month. I wanted to make sure that you're okay and to tell you how sorry I am. Mayor Hunter will be missed."

"Yep, it's really hard right now. He was my boss and also a really good friend," he slurred. He buried his head down in his folded arms on the table.

"I don't mean to disturb you, so I'll be going. I just wanted to offer my condolences."

"Thanks. I have a lot to think through. I lost a good boss and a mentor and more than a friend. I don't even know if I'll still have a job. It's hard grieving by your-self," he said without lifting his head.

She stood and patted his shoulder. "Take care of your-self. You don't have family nearby?"

"No, just a few friends. My family is from Nebraska, but we're not close."

"I'm gonna take off now. I guess I'll see you at the funeral."

He said something, but his arms and the table muf-fled it.

Delanie stopped by the bar on her way out. Waving the bartender over she asked, "Could you make sure that he gets a cab back to his place?" She pulled thirty dol-lars out of her purse and handed it to him. He nodded and took the cash.

"Thanks," she said.

Delanie made her way out of the bar. The night air and starry sky were refreshing after her heartbreaking encounter with Cooper. She felt bad for the young man who was grieving alone. Delanie imagined the scandal that would erupt when the news broke about the mayor's secret life. Not only would Cooper have to grieve for the loss of a lover, he would be dragged into the middle of a very public frenzy where the wife would look like the sweet, grieving widow.

She took a deep breath and walked to the alley next to the club. A dog barked. She looked out at the street in time to see a large truck cruise by. The plates matched the one that had driven John and her off the road. She shivered and quickened her pace. She didn't catch her breath until she started the Mustang and locked all the doors. It was time to see what Duncan knew about the owner of the blue truck who kept appearing all over town.

Delanie took several deep breaths to quiet the bats that were bouncing around her stomach. She told the Mustang to dial Duncan. She hoped he would answer. It was Halo Night, and he was funny about getting interrupted during his regular video game nights.

Delanie left a voicemail asking Duncan to call her as soon as he heard her message. She cruised the Downtown Expressway and the Powhite Parkway on her way back home. The reflection of the bridge lights twinkling in the inky black water distracted her. The river was pretty at night, and it had a strange, calming effect.

Delanie's encounter with Cooper and the blue truck sighting made her restless. She tried Paisley's cell phone only to get her voicemail, too.

Stopping at the gas station for a junk-food fix, Delanie headed home to see what was on her DVR.

DELANIE JUMPED WHEN she heard banging on her front door. She realized that she had fallen asleep during her marathon of reality TV shows. According to the clock, it was one-thirty.

Slipping into her fuzzy slippers, she pulled her robe on over her pink flannel PJs and headed for the living room.

Duncan stood under the small porch light. "What's going on?" she asked. She opened the storm door and pulled him in.

"I just got your voicemail. You sounded panicked, so I came right over."

"Four hours later," she said, plopping down on the couch.

"Sorry, Halo Night." He sank into the barrel chair in the corner.

"I saw the blue truck guy again tonight. Please tell me that you have info on the driver."

"Where did you spot him that time?"

"Outside Freeda's. I noticed him when I was leaving. I saw him the other day at the Treasure Chest as well."

Opening his phone, he moved around to find his notes. "He was easy to trace. The truck is registered to Kenneth Albert Payne, who owns Treez Lawn Service. His nickname is Tripp. Okay, so where else have you seen him?"

"John Bailey gave me the license plate number. I'm sure he's the one who ran us off the road, but I haven't been able to get close enough to see if the truck has paint from John's truck on it. And then I saw him cruising by Freeda's tonight when I went looking for Cooper Richardson."

"His father is a commercial real estate developer in Richmond. His mom, the former Caroline Reese Holbrook, is a popular interior designer and Richmond socialite. Tripp's another trust fund baby."

"What else do we have on this guy? There's got to be a connection to the rest of our story." She curled her legs under her on the couch. "I've spotted him while investigating the mayor for Chaz and during a visit with Johnny V."

"Sorry. I was out of pocket for most of the night. That's about all I have so far, but I'll keep looking. We'll find out what's out there. I better get going since Margaret's waiting on me at home. She can't sleep when I'm out."

Not likely. Delanie decided not to make a derogatory comment about Margaret to Duncan. He always got defensive if anyone mentioned how much he babied his bulldog. "Okay. Thanks for all you've done. At least we know who we're dealing with." She followed him to the front door.

Turning to face Delanie in the doorway, he said, "Be careful. You've got someone's attention. And we need to figure out why." He hesitated for a moment, standing close to her face.

She smiled, and he took a step back. Delanie shut and locked the door behind the computer whiz.

Delanie poured a glass of milk and grabbed two cookies to calm her jangled nerves. After the last chocolate chip disappeared, she wiped up the crumbs and crawled into bed. There had to be some connection to Tripp's lawn service, the mayor, and Chaz. But how did John Bailey fit into all of this? And why did she notice Tripp first near Amelia County? That was nowhere near Chaz's territory.

Delanie tried to drift off to sleep, but she tossed and turned most of the night. After getting up twice, she gave up on sleep at about four o'clock and headed for the kitchen to write down anything that she could think of that related to Tripp, Chaz, and John Bailey. She hoped something new would jump out if she put her notes on paper.

TWENTY

DELANIE TRIED ON five outfits before deciding on a short-sleeved aqua top with a white shrug and jeans. For a little flair, she quickly painted her toenails to match her top and new platform sandals. The cell phone rang, but she couldn't find it under the pile of clothes on her bed. Letting the call go to voicemail, she checked her latest outfit in the mirror and glanced at her watch. Eight minutes to get on the road or she'd be late for dinner at John's house. But she had to find her phone first.

While her toes finished drying, she wondered if this could be the night. Then she worried whether this *should* be the night. In her eight years as a private investigator, she had never had any kind of personal involvement with a client or subject of an investigation. She had almost convinced herself that John Bailey wasn't Johnny Velvet and, therefore, not part of her work. Delanie slipped on her sandals and headed for Amelia County. After she passed the residential and business areas on Hull Street Road, she sped up to sixty and listened to her voicemails through the radio. They were all from a frantic Duncan with the order to call him immediately.

"Dial Duncan cell," she said to the car. She closed the passenger window, so that she could hear him.

After one ring, Duncan replied breathlessly, "It's

about time. I've been trying to get you all afternoon. I found the missing link."

"Well, then," she snickered, "they'll hang your picture right next to Darwin's."

"You'll want to hear this," snapped Duncan.

"Sorry. What did you find?" she asked.

"Yearbooks. I was about to give up, but I found it in St. Martin's Middle School yearbook, the 1992 edition. Tripp Payne was designated as the Class Clown. And Patrick Rollins Hunter was chosen as Most Likely to Succeed. He's the mayor's youngest child."

"Interesting. But how did you get their middle school yearbook?"

"There's a website with a ton of them online. But wait, there's more! There's also a photo of a very sullen Chaz Wellington Smith in his best Goth garb in the grade ahead of Payne and Mr. Mayor's son. He looks radically different with black hair. He looked surly, but not like he does now with that tattoo."

"Well, now. It's a rather small world. Duncan, you are amazingly awesome as usual. I can't live without you. I'm on my way to Amelia County. I'll check on Chaz first thing tomorrow. If he's withholding information, I might slug him."

Duncan let out a heavy sigh. "Be careful," he said in a voice that was less enthusiastic than before.

"I will. Will you be in the office tomorrow?" she asked, passing a white sedan near the Amelia County line.

"Yep. Not sure when. Probably by the afternoon. See you soon."

"Bye, Duncan. And thank you again. I appreciate all you do."

"Yeah, yeah. That's what you tell all the guys," he said and hung up.

Tripp, the mayor's son, and Chaz had attended the same small, private school. Too much of a coincidence. Delanie wanted to know more about the friendships or rivalries. There had to be more to this. She would call Chaz's lawyer in the morning to see about how to get in touch with her client. Chaz needed to spill the beans about his connection to Tripp Payne.

Delanie pulled to the end of John's driveway next to the white farmhouse. A few moments later, she tapped lightly on the front screen door. The main door was open, giving her a view of the dark hallway to the kitchen.

"Come on in," said John from somewhere inside the house.

"Hi." She stepped inside the cool interior of the front room.

"I'm back here in the kitchen getting ready to throw stuff on the grill. Do you want something to drink?"

"That would be nice," she said, following his voice to the kitchen.

"Chardonnay, iced tea, or lemonade?"

"Wine, please. How have you been? It feels like forever since I've seen you."

He put the bottle and her glass on the butcher-block counter and hugged her. "Good. I know. It's been a while since we've connected. How's work?"

"Good." She leaned into his T-shirt that smelled like his soap and his cologne. She wrapped her arms around him and rested her head on his shoulder. To Delanie, this was what a date was supposed to feel like.

He was the first to move a few minutes later. "I need to put the meat on if we want to eat any time soon."

"Can I help with anything?"

"There's a fruit salad in a container in the fridge if you want to put it in a bowl. Now, you know that most of my culinary secrets come from the grocery store," he said with a wink.

"Hey, it's in your bowl, so that counts as homemade for me." She took the red ceramic dish. He took a plate of steak kebobs out the kitchen door. Delanie heard the back screen door slam, and she fought the urge to rummage through his house while he was gone. She reminded herself that tonight wasn't about business.

John returned as she snapped the lid of the container shut and put the extra fruit salad back in the refrigerator. "All done. It looks good."

John stacked the plates, silverware, and sides on a large wooden tray. "Grab your glass and my beer, and we can wait for the kebobs on the deck."

Making their way through the dark screened-in porch, Delanie followed John around to a newish deck that faced the barnyard and the fields. Delanie sunk into a canvas chair facing the paddock. The steak smells and the cooling twilight created a wonderful summer backdrop. Myrtle and Stewart, the alpacas, wandered out, and the fireflies began their dance. The tree frogs even tuned up for the evening.

"They're adorable. They have the prettiest eyes. Hi, Myrtle. Hi, Stewart," she said as she waved to the curious alpacas.

John clicked his tongue, and Myrtle and Stewart's ears

perked up. "They're mostly nosy, but they're fun to have around."

After dinner, John brought out a lemon chess pie. Before he cut slices, he flipped a switch that turned on hundreds of white lights on the small trees and hedges between the house and the barnyard. The lights outlined the fence line and the edge of the deck.

"Ooooh, it's lovely," Delanie said. "It looks like Christmas."

"I'm glad you like it." He cut the pie and poured iced tea for both of them.

"And I'm impressed with the lemon chess pie. Did they have that in California?"

"They have everything in California, including Southern desserts."

"Dinner has been wonderful. Thank you."

"Hey, that's nothing. Wait for the dancing."

After a quiet dessert in the summer twilight, she said, "That pie was absolutely delicious. Thanks."

Getting up to clear the table, John motioned for her to stay seated. "I've got this. I'll be back in a few, so just relax."

"Thanks." The backyard looked like fairyland with all of the white lights. She wondered how long it had taken him to string all of them. He was full of surprises.

Her date, the twinkle lights, and the wine combined to put Delanie in a mellow place. She couldn't wait to see what else he had planned.

When John returned, he turned up a slow song on his phone and said, "How about that dance?"

"Why, I do believe I will," she said with an exaggerated Southern accent. "Mr. Bailey, you have a lovely place here. This has been the perfect summer night, and I'll be sorry for this evening to end." He pulled her closer and kissed her long and gently. Delanie hoped he didn't feel her knees tremble.

They continued to kiss and dance long after the song ended and moved on to whatever was next on the playlist.

John pulled away and held her chin in his hands. "The evening doesn't have to end. You're welcome to stay."

She nodded, and he cradled her hand and led her inside. Delanie wasn't paying attention to his house on this trip. She hadn't dated anyone in a long time, and John Bailey made her feel like a teenager again.

Leaving a trail of clothes to the dark bedroom, Delanie slid under the comforter, and John followed close behind.

TWENTY-ONE

DELANIE WOKE TO chicken noises and the sun peeking through the white sheer curtains. She took note of John's room for the first time. It had a queen-sized bed with a navy comforter. A tiny dresser and mirror were between two narrow windows, and a side chair sat alone, covered with a pair of jeans and a balled up T-shirt. The room looked like something in a 1960s sitcom with the sliding closet doors. No remnants of an '80s rock 'n' roll life appeared anywhere.

She slid out from under John's arm, grabbed her shirt and the rest of her clothes, and slipped into the bathroom.

For a bachelor's bathroom, the absence of clutter was striking. The floor-to-ceiling pink ceramic tile reminded Delanie of the bathroom in the house where she had grown up. She washed up in the old-fashioned, pedestal sink. Checking in the medicine cabinet, the PI in her rarely rested. Delanie chided herself for being here at all. She had spent an incredible night with John, and she hoped it would lead to more time together.

She ignored John's brush and toothbrush that were lying on the shelf above the toilet. She knew she should have taken them to compare with Emily Mercer's DNA sample. She felt guilty, but she pushed the work thoughts to the back of her mind.

Delanie dressed quickly, ignoring thoughts of the art student in Chicago and if this John was the girl's father.

Returning to the bedroom, she gently shook John. He rolled over, and she kissed him on the forehead. He pulled her in close and kissed her back.

"Good morning, sunshine."

"Good morning. I had a wonderful evening. I haven't had an extended date in a very long time."

"I'm glad you stayed. Where are you off to now?"

"I've got to check in at work. There's an assignment that's due soon, and I still have some more work to do on another project."

"You sure you have to leave now?" he asked, and he kissed her again. "I was going to make my sensational pancakes and feed the critters."

"Hmmmmm! You make a compelling argument to stay. I guess I could be a little late."

"Give me a second to shower, and I'll meet you in the kitchen."

"Deal." He kissed her again.

Delanie wandered down the hall. She had two other rooms with shut doors to explore on the way to the kitchen. And then there were the rooms upstairs. Swallowing the urge to snoop, she went straight to the kitchen and stayed put.

By the time John appeared, Delanie had the coffee-maker chugging.

"Caffeine will be ready in a minute," she said as he kissed the top of her head.

Pulling out pans and utensils, he occasionally called out ingredients that he needed her to get.

Impressed by his control of the kitchen, Delanie

plowed through the pancakes and fruit with pineapple juice and coffee when he set the food on the table.

After his second cup of black coffee, John said, "Well, do you want to meet the barn inhabitants, or do you have to leave?"

"I can hang out for a little while longer. And I'd like to see Myrtle again."

Stopping on the way out to slip on work boots, John held the door for Delanie. Her shoes weren't exactly designed for farm tours, but they would have to do.

She spent the morning with John feeding the chickens, alpacas, cow, donkey, barn kitties, and his pack of crazy dogs, while thoughts of Duncan, Chaz, and the blue truck guy slipped to the recesses of her mind. But she knew it was just a brief reprieve. The investigation would dominate her thoughts as soon as she backed out of his driveway.

WHILE SORTING THROUGH two piles of mail that were threatening to fall over and out of the box on her desk, Delanie heard the office front door open, and then the metal scraping sound of it closing again.

"Dunc?" she yelled.

After no answer, she walked to the tiny kitchen, where she ran into the back of Margaret.

"Hey, sweetie," she said, scratching behind the English bulldog's ears. "Where's your daddy?" Delanie heard shuffling in Duncan's office, so she followed Margaret down the hall.

"Hey, there. What's up with you?"

"Nothing," he said without looking up from his laptop on the desk. "Long night."

"I made strong coffee earlier," she said, pointing to the kitchen. "It's the good kind. I'm gonna set up camp in the conference room to try to figure out some of this Tripp the Tree Guy stuff. Do you have some time to talk it through with me? I could use your help."

"I guess," he said, rummaging through his black messenger bag. "I'll be there in a minute." He didn't look at her, and he slammed a book and his bag on the desk.

Delanie wasn't sure what was bothering Duncan. With him, it could be just about anything. Before she could think about what to do about her partner, her cell rang. "Falcon Investigations."

"Delanie Fitzgerald, please," said the deep male voice with the slight New Jersey accent.

"This is Delanie."

"Ms. Fitzgerald, this is Rick Dixon, Chaz Smith's attorney. I'm returning your call," he said. It sounded like he was flipping through papers.

"Yes, Mr. Dixon. I've done some research for Chaz, and he said for me to call you to find out the best way to contact him or to get information to him."

"I know who you are. Chaz raves about your investigative skills." After a pause and a noise that sounded like slurping, the attorney continued. "He's been moved for his safety to a facility in Hopewell. The police wanted to ensure that he's not in with the general population. He's got a lot of people in Richmond who don't like him right now. He can make a limited number of calls, but he can't receive them. Do you have something you want me to pass on to him?"

"I had a few questions for him. I was hoping he could

tie up some loose ends. Could you ask him to call me when he can?"

"I can. Or you can come with me and see him yourself. I'm going down there tomorrow. Meet me at the front gate at two o'clock if you want to meet with him. Bring ID and dress frumpy."

"Thank you, Mr. Dixon. If anything changes with your appointment, please let me know."

"Yup," he said, clicking off.

By the time Delanie set up the conference table and poured two cups of coffee, Duncan and Margaret wandered in.

"Okay, what do we know about ole Tripp?" Delanie picked up a marker on the whiteboard tray and began to doodle.

"Kenneth Albert Payne, III owns Treez Lawn Service with his dad. And besides basing his company's marketing on a misspelling, he drives a honkin' blue Dodge truck. He comes from a well-to-do family. He attended the ritzy St. Martin's with the mayor's son and your dear friend Chaz," he said. Then he took a breath.

Delanie scribbled random facts on the whiteboard in a variety of colors. "Okay, so was Tripp friends with both of them? Did the mayor's kid and Chaz run around together? I'm going with the lawyer tomorrow to see Chaz. I don't know what I'll find out, but I'd like to know about the middle school friendships. And what kind of relationship they have as adults."

"Okay. Here's what else I've found on Tripp," he said, checking his phone. "Tripp lives in a condo on one of the greens of Wyndham. His father's listed on the tax assessment, and he's his partner on the business tax records. He had a juvenile record, but I couldn't find any details since the records are sealed, and they might also have been expunged. As an adult, he had two DUI arrests, though one was dismissed. Tripp also had an assault charge dating back to 2009 from a fight outside of a downtown bar. It looks like he got into it with a couple of frat boys. He completed an anger-management program as part of his plea to a lesser charge, and he hasn't been charged with anything since. He did, however, have about four or five parking and traffic tickets over the last ten years."

"Anything else?"

"He's had six complaints filed against Treez in the last three years. All were about the quality of his lawn or irrigation services. His company's gotten a bunch of nasty comments on the web about his service and his attitude. He's never been married. He likes outdoor sports and motorcycles. And there have been two complaints to his neighborhood association over the last two years. Both were related to wild parties or loud motorcycles. All of his taxes have been paid, and he's bounced a couple of checks through the years. That's about it."

"You've been busy. Thanks, Duncan. This gives us a pretty good idea of his background. I'm gonna do a little spying to see what I can see. Anything you want me to ask Chaz?"

"Nah," he said, picking up his laptop. "I've got some things to work on. I'll be in my office if you need me."

"Okay, thanks again." This helped create a picture of what they knew of Tripp Payne. He was trouble, and he tried to run them off the road. Somehow, he found her because of her association with Chaz. She needed to keep looking over her shoulder until she figured out what he was up to. Delanie stepped back to inspect the whiteboard filled with Tripp facts. Her hands were covered in blue ink.

Unable to wipe the marker off her fingers, Delanie walked down the hall to the tiny bathroom. While she was washing up, she noticed Duncan's toothbrush and floss on the counter. Squelching a guilty feeling that she wasn't being professional, Delanie pocketed his green toothbrush on her way out. This should give her a negative results report for Emily Mercer's test to send to Tish Taylor.

Slipping into her office, she shut the door and quickly packaged the toothbrush for the lab analysis. She felt another twinge of guilt when she left it in the box for the mail. She'd have to remember to get Duncan a new toothbrush.

TWENTY-TWO

DELANIE PARKED IN the lot under the Library of Virginia and rode the elevator from the dark parking garage to the entrance.

Climbing the staircase that dominated the lobby, she looked at the displays on her way to the stacks. This was Delanie's favorite library, and she felt fortunate to have it so close to home.

She made her way to one of the computer terminals and entered a request for both the local and Washington, D.C., newspapers for thirty days after Johnny Velvet's death. California didn't have its newspaper collection online, so she decided to see what the Virginia papers carried about the rocker's death.

Checking her texts and email, she waited for her request to be processed. When her name appeared on the monitor, she retrieved the boxes of microfilm and found a viewer with a printer.

Delanie spent the next few hours paging through the papers from 1989. The headlines and the advertisements seemed like another world to her.

The papers covered Johnny Velvet's death on the day after the crash in a small article on the obituary page. The death of The Vibes' lead singer wasn't front page news in Virginia. She inserted her copy card to print the article. The coverage was smaller than what she had imagined. She found a story about the accident and a follow-up two days later that reported Jake had survived. But she found nothing about the funeral, investigation of the wreck, and any link to John Bailey of Amelia County. Delanie folded her printouts and returned the film. On a whim, she searched the catalog for Johnny Velvet. He appeared as a mention in several books. She printed the search results and spent the next hour looking for the references.

A large man with a ball cap and dark jacket breezed past her while she was perusing the shelves. His pace made her notice him. She peeked around the corner and through the bookshelves. Confident that it was a coincidence, she went back to her search.

After little else emerged about Johnny Velvet, Delanie took the stairs to the café for a sandwich and iced tea. Finding a metal table with four chairs under the library's massive steps, she sat down and checked her phone.

She texted Duncan, Nothing new at the Library of Virginia on JB.

Her phone dinged with his quick response, Odd that there aren't the expected paper trails.

She responded, Or information. I guess it's good for Tish. No one's written about it yet. I'm heading back to the office. See ya.

Margaret sends her love, he replied.

Delanie threw away her wrapper and cup. Stopping at the security desk, she asked the guard to validate her parking.

Out of the corner of her eye, she saw the guy in the dark hoodie and ball cap duck out the gift shop and hustle through the front doors. From the side, he looked a little like Tripp. She shook off the paranoia and headed to the elevator. But she did dawdle until several people arrived to accompany her to the dark garage.

Delanie bought a toothbrush and a prepaid phone at Walmart. Sitting in the Mustang, she added the minutes to the phone's account. When the phone activated, she dialed the number for Tripp's Treez and heard a voice-mail with a gravelly male voice. In her sexiest voice, she told Tripp's recording that she wanted a quote on some work and gave her new cell number.

The phone rang when Delanie was in a drive-through for iced coffee.

"Hello," Delanie said in her sultry, Southern voice.

"Uhh, this is Tripp from Treez Tree Service. I'm re-turning a call from a Melanie Johnson."

"This is she. Do y'all do landscaping for private res-idences?"

"Yup," he said. It was difficult for Delanie to hear him over traffic noise in the background. "We do landscaping, tree removal, and irrigation. Just about anything outside."

"Oooh, good to know," cooed Delanie. "I need to have my backyard landscaped. It might be nice to have an ir-rigation system too. How does this work? Do you give free estimates?"

"Yep. Give me your address, and I can come by later this week."

"I'm leaving soon to go out of town for a couple of weeks. Can we do something today or tomorrow? And do you provide references? Or like, could I go and see yards you've done? I'd like to get some ideas of what mine will look like when it's finished."

"I have references. I've also got before and after pictures."

"Where are you and your staff working today? Maybe I could stop in and take a peek?"

"I've got two crews out today. And I'm with one of 'em at a corporate office park right now. Let's make an appointment for tomorrow. And in the meantime, you can go to my website at trippingtreez.com to see pictures. There's some stuff clients have said about me there, too."

"Okay. But is there any way you could meet me this afternoon? I'm going to the spa tomorrow. Please, pretty, pretty, pretty please?" she whined in her best pouty voice.

"I've been on a job site all day. I don't have time to go home and change for a sales call," he said.

"That's okay. I'm sure you look fine the way you are. You sure sound fine on the phone. We can meet on my backyard patio, and I'll even provide the lemonade. No pressure, but I really need an estimate. I'd really like for y'all to start work while I'm out of town."

"Okay, where are you?" he asked with an agitated edge to his voice.

"I'm in Chesterfield County. It's 9272 Bethia Road off Winterpock Road. It's a blue cottage with white shutters," Delanie said, describing her neighbor's house across the street. The Evans family spent most of their summer in Maine, so she would have a clear view of their driveway from her house.

"Wow. That's kinda far. I guess I can be there in about an hour or so."

"Perfect. You are so great to do this. I can't wait to

meet you and see your pictures. I'll look at your website while I'm waiting." He grunted, and she clicked off.

Delanie drove home and turned the Mustang around in the driveway for a quick pull out. She parked it in the backyard where her car would be out of sight from the Evans's property. She could see the end of their driveway from her new parking spot. Getting tired of waiting for Tripp, she went inside the house.

It took Tripp almost two hours before he pulled the blue Ram truck into the driveway across the street. He was about six-foot-two, and he had the stocky look of a wrestler or a body builder. His sandy blond hair was thinning around his forehead, but he was definitely the same guy in the yearbook picture Duncan had found.

She watched Tripp bang on the front door of the Evans's home. He walked around the side yard and then he disappeared around back for a long time. Grabbing her purse, she slipped out the kitchen door. She pulled on a black ball cap and sank down in the front seat of the Mustang. The ring of her new phone broke the silence. She pressed a few buttons to switch it to vibrate. Changing her mind, she shut off the new phone and started the car.

When Tripp backed the Dodge out of the driveway, she idled slowly forward and followed behind him. She didn't want him to recognize her car.

She tailed Tripp back to Henrico County to a Lakeside neighborhood. When he pulled up in front of a beige bungalow behind several white work trucks with trailers, she cruised the street for an unobtrusive spot for lurking. Delanie found a good location around the corner, though she didn't need it for long. Tripp left again after getting out and talking to two men.

Delanie pulled out after the blue truck and followed Tripp to a corporate office park off Staples Mill Road. She spotted a small crew mulching flowerbeds. Watching him strike up a conversation with an older white male, she drove slowly by. She pulled into a nearby office complex where she could see his crew across the street and be ready to make her next move.

At the point where Delanie was about to give up, she saw Tripp climb back in the blue truck. He flipped off the man that he had been talking to and then sped away with squealed tires when he turned onto the main road.

She followed at a safe distance. After stopping for a six-pack and chips at a convenience store, Tripp jumped on the interstate and headed downtown. Following him from three cars back in the center lane, she watched Tripp make a quick exit at Second Street. She changed lanes quickly and continued to tail him. He zigzagged through one-way city streets to Cary Street. Her face grew hot when she saw Tripp park and head for the front door of the Treasure Chest.

Delanie had to find a way to get Chaz to talk about his relationship with Tripp. If he had something to do with Tripp running her and John off the road, she didn't know what she was going to do. She didn't like being played, and it was beginning to feel that way. It was probably good that Chaz was in jail.

TWENTY-THREE

LOOKING UP FROM the report she was proofreading the next afternoon for Tish Taylor, Delanie was a little surprised to see Duncan bouncing on his tiptoes in her doorway.

"Hey, there are two cops out front by the glass window, and it looks like they're coming in. Can you handle whatever it is? Margaret and I will be back later. We gotta go. See ya."

"Sure," she said. She wandered to the lobby. Duncan must have been watching the front door from his camera feed. Wondering why he had to rush off, she leaned on the receptionist's desk, and a tall officer in a green lieutenant's uniform tapped on the glass with one knuckle. The other officer drove off in his Chesterfield County car.

She unlocked the door, and her older brother Steve took off his hat and said, "Hey, D."

"Well, I'll be, if it's not my favorite cop. Come on in, Steve. Do you want something to drink?"

"Nah. What's new with you? Liz and the kids say hi and want to know when you're coming over for dinner."

"It's been busy, so dinner sounds good. Let me know what night works for y'all, and I'll bring dessert," she said, hugging him. "So, a dinner invitation brings you by my humble establishment?"

"Nah. It's been busy in my world too. I got a courtesy call from Richmond homicide a little while ago. They want to talk to you."

"Just talk?" she replied. "Should I be worried?"

"Got anything to be worried about?" he asked.

"Is that the cop talking or my smart-ass older brother?"

"Your brother, the cop," he said. "Who thought it would be nicer if I ferry you over to Richmond PD instead of having them show up at your place of employment or your house. You know, you're not exactly flying under the radar these days."

"Hey, it's nice to stand out," she said. "When are they expecting me? And I hope they asked nicely because I don't have to go and see them."

"They want to talk to you about your investigation. You don't have to go, but you may want to think carefully about your decision. You get points for the spirit of cooperation and all that."

"So, when are they expecting me to appear?"

"Now. Do you want to ride or follow?"

"I'll lead, but let me get my purse," she said.

After texting Duncan, she shooed Steve out of her lobby and stopped to lock the front door. "Where are we going?"

"They said to meet them on the third floor of the headquarters building on East Broad Street. You'll have to find your own parking."

"Because I'm not special like you," she said, pinching him lightly on the arm.

Delanie rolled out of the front parking lot in the Mustang with her police shadow behind her. She was thinking about what she would or should say at the police station when she looked up at a stoplight and noticed a blue Dodge truck two vehicles ahead of her. When the light turned, she stomped on the accelerator and squeezed the car into the left lane.

She caught her breath when she read Tripp's license plate. Delanie followed him for a mile or so until he exited Hull Street for Route 288 South. This was a different direction for Tripp. She almost trailed him, but the blue lights flashing in her rearview mirror made her think twice about bolting. She wondered if it was a coincidence that he was on this side of town or whether he was back to check out the fake address again. Her phone rang when she was deciding what to do next.

"Hello."

"What are you doing? You're not supposed to be talking and driving."

"You called me, Mr. Policeman. I saw someone I've been investigating, and he happened to go in the other direction. It's unusual for him to be on this side of town during the day."

"Pull over into that parking lot on the left," snapped her older brother. He clicked off the phone and made his siren chirp twice to punctuate his order.

Delanie rolled her eyes. She was in for another lecture from Lieutenant Fitzgerald.

"What is going on with you?" Steve snapped when he approached her car.

Lowering the window, Delanie smiled and said, "I was out for a nice ride downtown. I just happened to see someone who I was investigating. Like I said, it's odd that he's on this side of town. And I was curious, so I didn't want to lose an opportunity to see where he was going."

"What were you thinking, Delanie?"

"My client has been arrested for a murder he didn't commit. I've been doing a little research, and the guy in the blue truck keeps popping up. It seems he went to a private school with the victim's son and my client. He turns up way too often for it to be a coincidence, so he's my biggest lead right now. And thanks to you, I'll have to pick up the tail later."

"Quit with the *my client* sanitized version. I know it's Chaz Smith, and you're dancing around the mayor's murder. Chaz Smith is a scumbag. He's got a rap sheet a mile long, and he's been associated with prostitution, drug sales, and pornography. I don't know if I'd take him on as a client."

"You're a cop. You don't get to pick your clients. And the folks that you work with every day aren't always upstanding citizens either. You deal with every dirtbag that comes along. And I know he's a sleaze. I'm not always sure I can believe everything that he says, but he didn't kill the mayor. He was alibied by his staff. And he's a paying client."

"This isn't about me. You're the one traipsing around with a strip club owner who can't keep his big mouth shut. And being alibied by your employees is almost as good as getting a reference from your mother or your preacher. Everyone in prison claims he's innocent. *Everyone*. Delanie, the police have a reason to hold him. Plus, if they did let him out, he wouldn't be safe on the streets. This town is in mourning for its murdered mayor. Whatever your politics, he was a beloved father figure. Heck, he was a state legislator and served in the House of Representatives for two terms. He has friendships that go back decades and a pool of favors with every kind of politician and bigwig that you can imagine."

"Maybe that was his image on the public side. But I found something while I was looking into Chaz's complaints. The mayor was not what he seemed," she said, her voice dropping off to a whisper.

"What? A girlfriend?" he asked, leaning inside the Mustang.

"No, boyfriend," Delanie whispered.

"Delanie, you can't go making allegations, especially against people with his connections."

"Steve! I have video proof, and I was a witness to it. I had the mayor dead to rights. There was no question about it. The beloved mayor was leading a double life with a cute male staffer."

"What am I going to do with you?"

"Nothing. I'm a professional. I make a living doing this job, and I haven't done anything wrong. I appreciate you being the big brother, but you don't have to worry."

"No, I do have to worry about you. Because I keep getting calls from law enforcement about you."

"Twice in like four years, and both were related to my clients. It wasn't about me, and it's not like I'm a hooker or a junkie. This is a legitimate job, and I can pay the bills with it. I can take care of myself, Steve. Plus, you always said to fight for the underdog."

"Delanie, you give me more gray hairs than my kids do. I worry about you."

"Well, thanks, but I don't need you to worry. I'm okay, but tell Liz that I can always use an invitation to dinner."

"I know I'm not going to change your mind. I want you to be careful and not be sassy with the detectives. They're in the crosshairs on this one, and it probably wouldn't take much lip from you to end up sitting in jail."

"Okay, okay. About ready? I don't want this to be an all-day affair."

"Fine, head downtown this time to the headquarters building on East Broad Street, and no detours. I don't care if you see Santa Claus and the Tooth Fairy on the way. I'll meet you at the front door."

About twenty minutes later, she found Steve with his cool mirrored shades waiting on the sidewalk by the front door of the public safety building. They walked through the security checkpoint, and Steve pushed the elevator button for the third floor.

Exiting the elevator, Steve steered her down the hall to a receptionist's desk.

"May I help you?" the female officer behind the counter asked.

"We're here to see Detectives Hagar and Roth," he said.

"They are waiting for you down the hall. Third door on the left."

"Thank you," Delanie said. She followed her brother to where the police officer directed.

Steve knocked and opened the door after a muffled "come in" came from inside.

"Good afternoon. I'm Lieutenant Steve Fitzgerald, and this is my sister, Delanie Fitzgerald."

"Have a seat," the tall detective said. He was wearing a blue suit and standing at the whiteboard.

The former conference room was now a war room with boxes and coffee mugs scattered across the long oak table. Hundreds of photos dotted the wall across from the second detective.

"I'm Detective Ron Hagar," the tall one said. "This is Detective Mike Roth. Ms. Fitzgerald, we have a few questions for you that we hope will help with our investigation."

Delanie sat across from Detective Roth. From her seat, she could see Theatre IV's historic Empire Theatre and some of the galleries on Broad Street. Shopping or a gallery tour would be way more fun than sitting here answering questions about Chaz. But maybe she could get a bead on the investigation from their questions.

"Ms. Fitzgerald, we'd like to talk to you about Charles Smith," Detective Roth said.

"As you know, he's my client," she replied. She took a deep breath and exhaled. She hoped they wouldn't notice how nervous she was. She was determined that she wouldn't let them intimidate her, especially in front of Steve.

"Yes. We've talked to Mr. Smith multiple times and understand that he's retained your services. We'd like to hear your assessment of the events," Detective Roth said. His faux leather chair squeaked when he moved.

Delanie looked across the room at Steve who remained standing between the door and the wall of photos. His face darkened like he was trying to send her some telepathic message. She stared at him for a few seconds with what she hoped he would take as a glare and continued with, "Well. I don't want to violate any client confidences."

"There is no client privilege with private investigators," Detective Hagar huffed.

"I know. But as a good business practice, I try to be discreet." She shifted in her seat and continued. "I met Mr. Smith a few weeks ago. He was having problems getting permits for his new business on Broad Street, and he felt that the neighborhood association and several city offices were treating him unfairly. He wanted me to see what I could find out about his permits and applications."

"And?" Detective Hagar asked, shifting his papers on the large wooden table.

"I found some information and presented it to him. When he paid me, I thought the job was over."

"What kind of information?" Detective Roth asked.

"A report of what my partner and I found. Then, Mr. Smith contacted me again and asked me to research someone's background," she said, looking at the tall detective standing near Steve.

"Let's not be coy, Ms. Fitzgerald. He asked you to look into the mayor's personal life."

"Yes, he asked me to see what I could find out about some rumors. I presented him with my findings, and that was the end of our business relationship until Mr. Smith called me again."

"What else did he want?" asked Detective Roth.

"He had approached the mayor with a proposal, and it was interpreted as threatening. Then the unfortunate events with the mayor transpired. Mr. Smith called to tell me that he was innocent, and he wanted me to look into the events of this week."

"What exactly did you give Mr. Smith?" asked Detective Hagar.

"The first time, I presented him with a written report. The second time, I gave him a thumb drive."

"Do you have copies of those?" asked Detective Roth.

"Yes," she replied. "You can have them with a subpoena."

Steve glared at her, but she said nothing else.

"That can be arranged," Detective Hagar said. "How did Mr. Smith appear when he contacted you the third time?"

"I didn't see him that time. He called and sounded agitated. He indicated that he thought he would probably be arrested. And he was upset about the mayor's murder."

"Did you see him again?" Detective Hagar asked.

"Yes. He asked me to come down to his office. I talked with his staff who discovered the mayor in his Mercedes outside of Mr. Smith's establishment. We also went through surveillance footage to see who drove the car in front of his business. Several of his employees were able to alibi Mr. Smith."

"We know. We've been to the Treasure Chest, too. Several times actually. We'll submit the paperwork and have the subpoena to you in the next day or so for your documents and files. Thank you for coming in. We'll be in touch. And thanks, Lieutenant Fitzgerald."

Steve nodded and opened the door. Rising from her seat, Delanie followed her brother down the hall. They rode the elevator to the lobby in silence.

Delanie broke the tension when they were on the sidewalk. "Well, that didn't take long. I'm headed back to work. I guess Richmond PD will be in touch if they want anything else. I look forward to getting their love note for the copies of my files."

"Delanie!"

"Don't start," she interrupted. "I appreciate all of your help, but we don't agree on everything. We see things from different perspectives. I do what I have to do. And you have your own way. But I love you."

He shook his head and put on his sunglasses.

"If you're not too mad at me, text me and invite me over to see Liz and the kids. The kids are growing up too fast, and I miss you guys."

He patted her arm and nodded. Steve turned and walked toward the law enforcement parking lot.

"Hey, Steve," she yelled. When he turned around, she said, "Thanks!"

He smiled and sauntered toward his squad car.

TWENTY-FOUR

DELANIE PULLED HER Mustang into the lot of the regional jail in Hopewell where Chaz temporarily resided. Rick Dixon had told her to wait out front until he arrived. She crossed the cement footbridge, walked to the entrance, and stood under a green aluminum awning.

Dressed in a black outfit that made her feel as demure as a nun in a habit, she had pulled her hair back in a bun. Her sensible shoes rounded out the outfit and made her look nondescript. With no jewelry and only mascara for makeup, she hoped her look was low key enough for the jail and Chaz's lawyer.

After a twenty-minute wait in the summer heat, Delanie spotted a man with an expensive suit stepping out of a classic Corvette. Guessing he was Rick Dixon, Delanie took a couple of steps toward the attorney.

He didn't speak until he arrived at the security door at the front of the building. "Darcy?"

"Delanie, Delanie Fitzgerald," she replied.

"Nice to meet you," he said, holding the door for her. "Follow me. I'm hiring you, so hold this for me." He handed her a dollar. Not waiting for a response, he strode down the corridor.

At the security checkpoint, Delanie rooted through her purse for identification. "Good afternoon. I'm Attorney Rick Dixon. I'm here to see my client, Charles

Wellington Smith. This is my private investigator." He pointed at Delanie and flashed his driver's license.

She handed her identification to the male guard, who made notations on a clipboard. A few minutes later, he said, "Go down through the metal detectors to the end of the hall to the door with the orange sign."

"Thank you," Delanie said as she took back her ID. She put Rick's money in her jacket pocket. *This is going to cost him way more than a dollar.*

At the end of the hall, they found a large steel door with a window by the orange sign. Rick opened it, and Delanie followed him into a waiting room. Seats facing small cubicles and a large glass window ran the length of the room.

Clearing his throat, Rick said to the guard at the desk, "Excuse me. I'm Rick Dixon, and this is Delanie Fitzgerald. We're here to see Charles Wellington Smith."

"Yes, sir." The female guard in a uniform tapped something into her computer. "Please be seated in cubicle nine. Someone will bring him out shortly." She pointed to the last open space in the row. "When he arrives, just push the speaker button when you want to talk."

Delanie and Rick settled in the plastic chairs. Delanie squirmed in her attempt to get comfortable. After a short wait, a guard led Chaz through a door into the room on the other side of the glass. She was surprised at the transformation of the strip club owner who stood before them in the orange jumpsuit. His face looked tired, and he had bed head.

Rick was the first to speak again when he jumped to push the square button on the counter. "Chaz, how are you?"

climbed into the Mustang. Pushing the button to drop the windows, she blasted the air conditioning until the car cooled off.

Delanie spent the long ride from Hopewell thinking about Chaz. Every other time she encountered him, she couldn't shut him up. He knew Tripp. And after today's interview, she was convinced there was more to the relationship than he let on. Chaz was being evasive. She hoped Tripp wasn't the hired muscle for Chaz's extracurricular activities.

PULLING HER SUNGLASSES down to block out the last of the evening sun, Delanie decided to give up on her spur-of-the-moment stakeout in front of Cooper Richardson's condo. She started the car about the same time she saw the mayor's former aide exit the building and walk toward the remains of the historic canal. Delanie angled the car into traffic and followed him from the street.

Cooper Richardson didn't seem to be in any hurry. He ambled through the inner city park, bordered on one side by the canal and the other side by old warehouses that had been converted into upscale dwellings and shops.

Debating whether or not to park and follow Cooper on foot, Delanie froze when she saw a blue truck zoom by in the left lane and cut off the car in front of her. She slammed the brakes to avoid the rear bumper of the car ahead of her. The big truck had Tripp's personalized plates. Now she had the fun of watching two marks.

Delanie watched Tripp pull off about a block away in an on-street parking spot. She followed Cooper on foot after he jumped out and walked toward the Haxall

Towers. When he got to the building's double doors, he disappeared through the main entrance. Tripp was close behind. Delanie saw a hostess seat Cooper at a table on the outdoor patio under a maroon umbrella that fluttered in the late afternoon breeze. Then Tripp entered the building, taking a seat by himself. At about the time the waitress brought Cooper a second drink, Tripp exited the main door and headed for his truck.

Since Cooper was dining alone, and it didn't look like he had anywhere to be, Delanie picked Tripp to tail. She wondered why he gave up following the mayor's aide. Tripp headed to his vehicle. She jogged to her car and whipped it around so she could follow the big truck.

She tailed him through the narrow downtown streets until he pulled into the lot of the Treasure Chest. She texted Chaz's lawyer and her brother Steve to let them know about her latest Tripp sighting. Then she texted Duncan that she had been following Tripp who was following Cooper. She didn't think hanging out at the Treasure Chest again would yield any new clues.

TWENTY-FIVE

DELANIE DROPPED HER purse on the vinyl seat and slid into the booth across from her reporter friend, Ami Lawrence. The converted storefront made a long and narrow establishment, and the tall wooden booth made their area seem like a tiny room. The booths ran parallel to the lunch counter and kitchen.

"Hi. Great choice for lunch," Delanie said.

Ami looked up from her menu.

"It's been one of those weeks. I needed some good ole Southern comfort food." She tucked her long blond hair behind her ears.

"I hope you haven't been waiting long. I got tied up on some phone calls after we talked." Delanie flipped through her menu and tried to decide on her lunch order.

"No. It took me a little while to find parking on this end of Broad Street." Ami put down her menu and opened a portfolio, and a waitress took their drink and food orders.

Ami said in almost a whisper, "I finally got my editor to agree to a different angle on the mayor's story based on the information that you found. This one doesn't portray him as a saint and the city's savior. My editor was interested in the edgy side of it, but he's been quietly checking to see what kind of effect it will have in the city. We know it's going to be a shock to the conservative community when it learns their hero had a secret life that was never talked about. We compromised, and he agreed to run the article after the funeral. Hopefully, some of the media hype will die down soon. Thanks to you, ours will be the only story with this angle. This is going to be a big one for me."

"I'm glad my research could help you. I know it's going to be a surprise to a lot of people. I hope you don't get a huge backlash."

"We like shock and awe. And hopefully, we don't scare off our big advertisers. The story will be out in next Wednesday's edition. I brought you a preview copy. I wanted to thank you for all of your help."

"Hey, it's the least I can do. I owe you so many favors."

"Delanie, we're ready for the firestorm. This is not the conventional image that the mayor sold his constituents, or the picture that his family presents. Plus, there's the son-in-law congressman in the mix. None of them is going to like this. But it's not the only controversy that my little paper has stirred up over the years."

"It's about time the truth got out. Be careful though. There are a lot of crazies out there."

"That's par for the course. We get at least two or three bomb threats a year. We wouldn't be doing our jobs if we didn't offend someone."

"I wish you could have seen the mayor's assistant after the murder. It was heartbreaking," Delanie said.

The waitress brought their lunch orders.

After she left, Ami said, "I heard the mayor's assistant is a nice guy and good at what he does. He didn't seem to be a fit in with ultraconservative politics." After a couple of bites of gooey mac and cheese, Ami continued. "Hopefully, he'll move on to another campaign and candidate."

They finished lunch, and each had a serving of the restaurant's famous banana pudding for dessert. Delanie and Ami parted on the sidewalk.

"Thanks, again," Delanie said.

"Ditto. I'll call you next week and let you know how it goes. Oh, here's your copy. Just keep it under wraps for a couple days."

"Thanks, I can't wait to read it," Delanie said, hugging her friend in the bright afternoon sun. "Good luck! Wear your thick skin and big girl pants. You are definitely in for an interesting ride."

Delanie sat behind the wheel of the Mustang and blasted the air conditioner to get rid of the summer heat. She read Ami's article. When she finished, she carefully refolded *Essence Weekly* and put it on the front seat to show Duncan. Ami had found several folks to corroborate Delanie's video of the mayor and Cooper, even though they wouldn't ever have said a word when he was alive.

Delanie thought it odd that she hadn't received a subpoena from the police yet. As far as she was concerned, Richmond PD could read about the mayor next Wednesday in *Essence Weekly* like the rest of the city.

On her way to the office, the phone rang.

"Delanie, it's Chaz. I wanted to thank you for coming by to visit me yesterday. It was good to see you."

"I wish it could have been under better circumstances," she said.

"I'm sorry that you left mad. I was so pissed at Rick that I couldn't think straight, and I didn't feel like talking. This place is awful. You can't even imagine what goes on here. And I've seen a lot of crazy over the years. Can you talk now?"

"Are you going to be straight with me, Chaz? I can't help you if you don't tell me the whole story. I don't have time to mess around."

"Not a problem. I felt bad since you've always been good to me. What do you want to know?"

"How do you know Tripp Payne?"

"I've known him since middle school, but I haven't seen him in years. He's been a toady for the mayor's son Patrick since sixth grade. He's a skank. Plus, he has no brains or personality. The only things he had going for him were that his parents had money, and Patrick Hunter graced him with his presence. I tried to steer clear of that bunch as much as possible."

"Really?"

"Yep, why?" he asked.

"I've tailed him to the Treasure Chest several times. Listen, Chaz, I really don't have time to play. Is Tripp a friend, or do you do business with him? Just tell me the truth. Did you hire him to take care of things for you?"

"Delanie, no, I swear," he whined. "He's bad news. He's been trouble since I first met him. I can't help it if he patronizes my establishment. A lot of people go to my club. I don't know everyone by name or face. But I can guarantee you that I haven't talked to him in at least ten years. If I've seen him recently, I didn't recognize him. He's dangerous with that temper of his."

"Really, Chaz? You're warning me away for my safety and not because you don't want me to discover something?"

"Delanie, he went to jail a couple of times as a juvenile. But somehow, things always got swept under the rug. He attacked a math teacher in class once. He broke the guy's nose and arm before they could pull him off. He got some girl knocked up in school, but that got taken care of, too. He ran with Patrick Hunter's crowd, and stuff didn't stick to him. I think he got kicked out of college too. Delanie, I've got to go. Be careful. He's nuts. Oh uh, hey, I appreciate you looking into this for me."

"Take care, Chaz. I'll call Rick Dixon if I find anything."

"Thanks. I'll talk with you later."

Delanie clicked off. She had the feeling he wasn't lying, but something wasn't quite right about Chaz and Tripp.

TWENTY-SIX

THE NEXT DAY, Delanie disconnected the call and drummed her purple fingernails on the steering wheel. Before she could think more about the last call, her phone rang again.

"Hello, Dunc," she said as she clicked the button on her steering wheel.

"Hey, what's up?"

"Are you coming in?"

"I was, but I got an odd call from a prospective client." She continued to drum her nails as she talked.

"How weird?"

"He works at an art gallery, and he thinks one of his employees is stealing from him. He wants a discreet investigation."

"So?"

"He was evasive. There's something he's not telling me. Then he asked if I could meet him in an hour at Maymont."

"You want me to go with you?"

"No. I'll be okay. I told him I would meet him outside the gift shop. I want to get there before he does to stake out the area."

"Be careful. Call me when you leave."

"Yes, Dad."

"See ya," he said as he clicked off.

About twenty minutes later, Delanie parked the car

under an old oak with branches that spanned five cars. She locked the car and retrieved her briefcase from the trunk. Maymont's gates looked like they belonged on palace grounds. She followed the path that slithered through the estate and gardens, stopping in front of the old mews and carriage house from the former Dooley estate that served as the gift shop and visitors center. Finding a wooden picnic table under some oaks, she took a seat and checked her email.

Twenty minutes later, she saw a distinguished gentleman in a dark suit approach. His eyes darted around the park. She watched as he stopped in front of her. His thin frame cast a tall shadow that covered her.

He hesitated for a second or two and then said, "Ms. Fitzgerald?"

"Yes."

"I'm Arthur Thornberg. We spoke on the phone."

"It's nice to meet you, Mr. Thornberg. Have a seat. How can Falcon Investigations help you?"

"I'm in charge of a gallery, and I think someone is taking art from our collection," he said, shifting his weight from foot to foot.

"What's missing?"

"We catalog everything that goes in or out for any reason. I had my suspicions, so I did some checking. I found some items that were sent to storage, but they can no longer be accounted for. Then I discovered that more items had disappeared over the last two years," he said, jingling the coins in his pants pocket.

"Who had access to the items?"

"Two staff members are in charge of sending and receiving. I want your firm to look into this and report your findings to me. If my suspicions are correct, then I'll contact the authorities. Here," he said, handing her an index card.

Delanie took the white card and read the black print. Each side had a name, social security number, and contact information. One was for Tyler Peterson, and the other was Shelley Tillsley.

Delanie fished in her purse for her notebook and pen as Thornberg continued, "Tyler Peterson has been employed with us for five years. He reports to me, and the department's administrative assistant is Shelley Tillsley."

"What's missing?"

"A Victorian vase, a small watercolor, a silver necklace, two silver serving spoons, and four African masks."

"Do you have pictures of the missing items?"

"Here's a list of the items and their values. I can email photos to you later."

"Okay, my partner and I can help you with this. Here is our contract and fee and expense structure. We require a fifteen percent deposit. From what you've said today, it looks like it will be four or five days of research. We usually send a written report with pictures or videos. Do you have an email address where I can reach you?"

"Yes," he said, taking the folder she handed him. He flipped through the contents and then reached in his jacket pocket.

Sitting down on the picnic bench, he looked at the fee chart and wrote a check. Then he signed the contract. Handing the pages to her, he said, "Here. I wrote my personal email on that page. I look forward to seeing what you find." Then he rose and followed the path back to the park's gate.

Delanie tailed him. She was curious about his caginess and agitation. She watched him climb into a black BMW 550i, parked at the other end of the lot from her car.

Trailing him from a few car lengths back, his sedan hugged the curvy roads surrounding Maymont and Byrd Parks. He traveled through neighborhood streets filled with once elegant homes on his way to Broad Street. She followed him through the city until he made a quick right on Arthur Ashe Boulevard, and then another quick turn into a lot beside the Virginia Museum of History and Culture and the Virginia Museum of Fine Arts.

When she watched him pull into the parking deck and head for the staff parking area, she backed her car out of the gate and headed to the office.

"Dial Duncan cell," she commanded the car.

A few seconds later, she heard, "What's up?"

"I met with Mr. Thornberg."

"Good or bad?"

"Just weird. He acted extremely nervous. He told me he worked at an art gallery. I shadowed him when he left Maymont, and he went to the art museum."

"Maybe he's a big art fan?"

"Possibly. But he pulled into the staff parking area of the deck. I'm going to call him when I get in. He's got to level with me if he wants us to continue with his case."

"Okay. Margaret and I will be here if you need anything."

"See you soon," she said.

Thirty minutes later, Delanie dropped her purse on

her desk and booted her laptop as Duncan and Margaret stuck their heads in her office.

"Hey," she said, as she plopped in her chair.

"Hello. What's up with the art guy named Art?"

She laughed. "He goes by Arthur, and he gives me a weird vibe. He's way too jumpy. Here are the names he gave me. I'm gonna call him."

"I'll be right back. I need to get my laptop."

Delanie punched in the number for her new client. She pressed the speaker button as Duncan took up residence in her guest chair.

On the tenth ring, they heard, "Hello."

"Mr. Thornberg, this is Delanie Fitzgerald. I had a couple of follow up questions for you."

They heard some shifting and a door close. "Okay. Any problems?"

"No. I thought I heard you say you managed a gallery in Richmond."

"Yes."

"I didn't get the name of your shop."

He cleared his throat and paused. "I'm affiliated with the Virginia Museum of Fine Arts. I want to keep this as quiet as possible. I want proof that someone is stealing before I make a formal accusation. I don't want to ruin a career if I'm mistaken."

"Do you think you're mistaken?"

"Uh, no."

"Okay. My partner and I will do some research and give you a report in a few days."

"Thank you. Use this number to contact me. Please don't call my work number." He disconnected the call.

"Well, at least that explains his jumpiness," she said to Duncan.

"Give me a minute or two. Let's see what I can find in the big, tangled web."

"I'm going to get a drink. Can I get you anything?"

"Water, please," he said, tapping his laptop keys.

By the time she returned with the two bottles and cookies, he said, "Okay. Tyler Peterson is thirty-two and single. He grew up and went to college in Pittsburgh. He lives in the posh condos at Short Pump. He has one ex-wife and no children. And he drives a black Jetta. Shelley Tillsley is forty and married with three kids. She likes quilting and her three cats, Sugar, Spice, and Mr. Jiggers. She lives in Brandermill with her cop husband. He's a detective in Henrico County."

"Hmmmm," she said, taking notes.

"Then there is your Arthur Thornberg, Director of Acquisitions for the VMFA. He's been there for fifteen years. He lives with his wife Jeanette in the Fan. He drives a big BMW, and they have two grown kids. He's on the Board of the Children's Museum, and his wife is heavily involved with charity work. And they own a golden doodle named Maximillian."

"What about tax assessments and net worths?"

Duncan clicked more keys as he poked around the darker parts of the Internet.

"The Thornbergs have about six years left on their mortgage. Their only income is his. They have about five thousand in credit card debt, and they have a mortgage on a second home in Nags Head. Shelley and her cop husband have twenty years left on their mortgage. They just refinanced. Their 2008 Honda is paid off, and they have a Ford truck. They have about a thousand dollars in credit card debt, and their home is assessed at a little over two hundred and sixteen thousand." He took a swig of his water and continued. "Tyler rents his condo for a hefty two grand a month. He owes three years on the Jetta. He has about thirty thousand in credit card debt and fifty thousand-ish in student loans."

"We'll start with Tyler," she said.

"Agreed. I'm gonna dig deeper later tonight. I wonder if he has any online websites to sell stuff. It may take some time."

"Okay. I'm going to trail him for a few days. Do you have a recent picture of him?"

"I knew you'd ask. I've printed what was on the web."

"Thanks."

"Come on, Margaret. Let's go get the printouts."

Delanie looked up the VMFA number and dialed it from her burner phone.

When the perky voice answered, she said, "Oh, hi. May I have Tyler Peterson's office, please?"

After a few minutes of classical music, she heard, "This is the office of Tyler Peterson. I am away from my desk or on the other line. Please leave a message, and I'll call you back. My office hours are eight to four-thirty on weekdays."

That told Delanie what she was looking for. She disconnected before the beep and went to see what Tyler looked like in person.

TWENTY-SEVEN

DELANIE FIDGETED IN the front seat of her car. The more she moved, the more the wire taped under her black dress crept up. She was waiting for Tyler Peterson to leave work. She had been following him for the past five days. On four occasions, he visited a restaurant and a bar downtown, and then he ended up at Habaneros near his condo. Then one night, he followed his same dinner routine, but ended up at the Treasure Chest. Great, another mark who frequented Chaz's establishment.

She started the car when she saw Tyler drive out of the staff parking at the museum. Following from a few car lengths back, she watched him find on-street parking next to Hometeam Grill.

Delanie checked her phone for the hundredth time as Tyler came out of the restaurant and jumped in his car. After stopping at a convenience store, she watched him hop on the interstate for a trip west. She followed him to his condo. He parked and trotted up the stairs with his briefcase and a case of beer.

About an hour later, she spotted him walking on the sidewalk toward his favorite bar, the same routine as the previous nights. Giving him time to get inside, she drove down the block and parked near the front of Habaneros. She fluffed her hair and grabbed her purse with the video recorder.

After being waved in by the bouncer, she edged up to the ebony bar and ordered a pinot grigio. Tyler was at the end of the bar talking to two young ladies. When the two women moved on, Delanie pressed the record button on the camera in her purse and approached. "Hi. How are you? Do you mind if I wait here for a few minutes for my friend? She's supposed to meet me here."

"No, problem. I'm Tyler. Your first time here?"

Delanie nodded. "I'm Tracie. This is a busy place. I thought we were going to meet here for drinks and then go to some club."

"You wanna grab a table while you wait?"

"That sounds nice. So, Tyler, what do you do?" she asked as she followed him to a small corner booth illuminated by a pendant light.

"I'm an art curator. I deal in antiquities," he said. "And what about you?"

"Oooooh. That sounds so exciting," she cooed. He smiled and leaned closer, and she continued with, "I'm an interior designer, and I'm new to the Richmond area. I've only been here a couple of months."

"Well, if you're interested, I can give you a tour. It's a neat city, and there are lots of places to hang out. Can I get you a refill on that?"

"I'm good for now, but maybe in a few minutes."

Delanie spent the next forty-five minutes listening to Tyler blabber on about his clients and his experience in the art world. From his rendition, he sounded like a cross between Picasso and Indiana Jones. He excused himself, went to the men's room, and then returned with two drinks.

"I think your friend ditched you," he said. This time, easing into the booth on her side and moving close to her.

"It looks that way. I haven't heard from her, so I guess I'll be heading out soon. It was really nice to meet you."

"Uh, if you don't have plans, my place is just around the corner. If you'd like to come up for a drink, I'll show you some of my collection."

"I guess," she said. *More time to snoop around and see if any of the items are there,* she thought. He scooted out of the booth, and she followed him to the front door and out into the warm summer evening. The Short Pump nightlife was in full swing. Throngs of singles and couples crowded the sidewalks, and all of the patio seating was at capacity.

She followed him through the crowd to his condo. He punched his security code and held the door for her. Delanie trailed him down the hall to number *143*. He unlocked the door and held it for her.

"Make yourself at home. I'm going to get some snacks," he said.

"Thanks. Your condo is lovely. It's right in the heart of all the nightlife here. I like that you're so close to everything," she said as she wandered through the aqua foyer to his living room.

She made sure to get a good shot of his African mask collection hanging over his couch. She was sure that several of them were on Arthur Thornberg's list of missing assets.

"Hey, Tyler," she said. "Tell me about your mask collection. These are fabulous. Where did you get them? I have a client, and we're doing his den in African décor. These would be perfect."

"Uh, I got them from one of my clients who goes to Africa every year. If you're interested, I can see if he has any more."

"That would be great. I would love three or four if the price was right."

"I'll see what I can do," he said as he came out of the kitchen with a tray of cheese and crackers. He put it on the coffee table and returned for a bottle of wine and two glasses.

"Here," he said, sitting on the couch. "In case you're hungry."

"Thank you," she said, nibbling on a piece of cheddar on a Ritz.

Tyler poured drinks and handed her one. Taking it, she sat next to him on the couch. He moved closer to her. Delanie, already bored with Tyler, started looking for an out. On a whim, she dropped her drink in her lap. The wine dribbled down and puddled on the carpet.

"Oh, I'm so clumsy. I am so sorry,"

"Oh, shit," he said. "I'll get some towels."

He returned a few minutes later and dabbed the carpet. After a pause, he handed her the wet rag. Delanie rolled her eyes and sopped up what had landed in her lap.

"This evening has been lovely, except for this. I think I need to head home and get this taken care of."

"You sure? I'm sure I can find you a T-shirt or something."

She rose. "Thanks, but I need to go home. Call me if you find more of those masks. They're great."

"Phone number?" he asked, handing her his phone.

She tapped in a number she made up and labeled

it, *Tracie Smith*. "Thanks for a fun evening," she said when she was finished. "See you soon?"

He nodded and let her out the door. When the door shut behind her, she switched off her camera and bolted for the car. She headed home for dry clothes and to draft her report about Tyler Peterson's mask collection.

TWENTY-EIGHT

BALANCING THE PLASTIC laundry basket on one hip, Delanie closed the dryer door with her knee. She hauled the clean clothes through the kitchen and living room on her way to the bedroom. Expecting John within the next hour, she glanced out the front window and stopped suddenly. She dropped the basket, dumping the warm contents on the living room rug.

Delanie ducked and crawled toward the plate glass window. Parked in the driveway across the street, Tripp's big truck straddled her neighbor's small driveway. The driver's door hung open, but there was no sign of the landscaper.

She crept back to the kitchen to find the disposable phone she had used to call him. There were four voicemails from Tripp, each angrier. She pushed the button to hear the last one.

"Melanie. Where the hell are you? I rearranged my freakin' schedule for you, and you're not answering my calls. You better call me back, bitch, or you'll be sorry. I don't have time to friggin' play."

Delanie turned off the phone. *Tripp sure knows how to cultivate client relationships.*

She staked out a spot in her living room near the big window where she would not be seen and kept checking her watch. Her legs felt tingly from crouching near the window. She saw Tripp come around the side of the Evans's home. He walked around the front of the house and opened the rural mailbox at the end of the driveway. Then he trotted across the street and opened Delanie's mailbox. It didn't look like he did anything except nose around. A few minutes later, he swung himself back into his truck and zoomed out of the driveway in reverse.

Delanie swallowed the urge to dash after him. She had only about fifteen minutes before John was supposed to arrive, and she didn't want to cancel on him at the last minute.

Forgetting about Tripp for the moment, Delanie picked up the laundry and straightened up. She had a sick feeling in her stomach that Tripp knew she posed as Melanie. *Why else would he snoop around in my mailbox too?* She shook off the creepy thoughts. She'd worry about Tripp and his threats later.

The doorbell interrupted Delanie's final touches on her makeup. Dropping the brush back into the plastic holder, she dabbed her lips, checked her look, and hurried to answer the door.

"Hi," she said, once she saw that it was John.

"Hi, back. You look nice," John said.

She held the door. "Would you like to come in?"

John stepped into the tiny living room and looked around the front room of her cottage.

"Nice house."

"Thank you. It's quaint and quirky. And it's just the right size for me."

"It's got a lot of character," he said.

"It was a Sears catalog house from the 1930s. The original owners ordered it and had it assembled. There are a couple of boards in the house that have the model information on them."

"I like it. I was thinking we could go to Seasons in Brandermill for dinner. Okay with you?" he asked. He looked at the pictures of her family on the wall across from the window. She felt a twinge of sadness when she looked closely at them. She missed her parents.

She shook off the melancholy. "Let me grab my purse."

A hostess seated Delanie and John on the split-level deck that overlooked the Swift Creek Reservoir. The developers designed the surrounding houses to blend in with the trees and the man-made lake. Watching the red and purple sunset, John and Delanie shared stuffed mushrooms and drinks. The warm breeze ruffled their hair and the white tablecloths. She enjoyed the view of the water and was content to simply be with John. There wasn't much conversation from him, but Delanie was getting used to that. She was intrigued by his mysteriousness, but she wondered if she could have a long-term relationship with someone who was so introspective and so much older than she.

Putting her fork down, Delanie broke the silence. "It's lovely out here. I could sit here by the woods and the water for hours," she said, watching an electric-powered pontoon boat cross the rippled lake. John smiled.

"So, what have you been up to lately?" she said. "I'm doing some research on a politician who's living a secret life. I'm amazed at the trouble he's going through to cover up what he doesn't want people to know. I don't think I could do it. I would find it hard to keep a major chunk of my life hidden."

John looked down at his plate. "Don't know much about that. I'm not that political, I just hang out with the farm animals in Amelia County."

She was going to push further on the topic, but he diverted his eyes again and dug into his steak. She let him eat in silence. His lack of conversation was getting frustrating. She turned her attention to the boats on the water.

John and Delanie finished their meal and left when the bats arrived to chase the mosquitos. She didn't have the energy to ask any more questions for him to dodge.

The sound of the truck tires crunching on her pea gravel driveway sounded louder when there was no conversation. He walked her up a short path to her porch and shifted from foot to foot as she unlocked the front door.

"Would you like to come in? If you still want dessert, I may have some Girl Scout cookies in the freezer."

"Tempting. I'd really love to, but I need to get home. I have a barn full of animals to feed, and they won't be very happy if I deviate from the schedule. I'll take a rain check on the cookies."

"The cookies are Thin Mints."

He smiled, and she continued, "Okay, well, thank you for a lovely evening. The dinner and sunset were amazing. Maybe next week, we could check out one of the parks or have a picnic or something."

"Sounds good." He leaned in and kissed her.

Not having any other plans for the evening, Delanie put on her favorite jammies and flipped open her laptop. She dropped on the bed and turned on the television for company until she fell asleep.

She jolted awake when she heard a series of loud pops and tires squealing. She glanced at the digital clock that showed *2:30*.

Padding to the front room, she flipped on the front-yard floodlights. All was quiet outside except for the crickets and the tree frogs. She stood in the dark for a few minutes watching for any movement out front. She wasn't sure if the noise was from outside or from the late night movie on TV.

Not noticing anything out of place or any movement, she returned to her room and turned off the television. She would look around outside when the sun came up.

TWENTY-NINE

HEADING TO THE kitchen for her morning ritual of coffee and emails, Delanie stopped in her tracks in front of the living room window. Skid marks streaked the road in front of the Evans's home. Her gaze darted to where the family's large mailbox had been. It now dotted the yard and driveway in three or four jagged pieces of crumpled metal.

Her thoughts jumped immediately to Tripp, and she regretted using the Evans's address for her ruse. She texted Duncan a picture of the debris, which looked like the remnants of a pipe bomb.

Delanie needed to get to the office, fast, but she made a quick stop at Lowe's to replace her neighbor's mailbox. Climbing out of the Mustang at the office, Delanie cradled the box of chocolate doughnuts and two iced coffees she had picked up at a doughnut shop on her way in. Tripp and his recent antics had created the need for sugar and caffeine.

Delanie flipped on the hallway lights and jumped when she almost stepped on Margaret.

"Hey, Baby. What are you doing lying here in the hall? Are you by yourself?"

Margaret opened one brown eye as Duncan came out of the restroom.

"Oh, hi, Dunc! I brought coffee and sugary sustenance. I need to update you on my psycho lead. Here, can you take these? I'll be right back; I need to go get the mailbox I left in my car. I want to open it and ask you some installation questions."

"Mailbox? Good morning to you too, Delanie. You know you're not normal," he said, shaking his head. "How do you get in these situations? And why is my green toothbrush yellow?"

"I'm just lucky, I guess. Oh, sorry! I sort of used your toothbrush for something else, and I replaced it with a new one. Don't be mad. I needed it in a pinch."

"I don't want to know."

Delanie returned a few minutes later with the mailbox that she set on the conference table. She and Margaret found comfortable seats and waited.

Reaching for a chocolate glazed doughnut, Delanie said, "Hey, Dunc. I wanna play these voicemails from Tripp for you. He's been by the Evans's house twice in the last two days. There have been six messages, and his anger's more apparent in each one."

She played the last one, "Call me, bitch, or you'll be sorry."

"Well, that was succinct, and he's so great with customers," Duncan said.

"And this is the one before it," she said as she pushed the button.

"All right, Melanie. I keep calling, and you don't answer. I did you a friggin' favor by coming out on the spur of the moment. If you know what's good for you, you'll call me back."

Delanie shook her head. "This guy is something else.

Do you have a camera I could borrow to see if he comes back when I'm not there?"

"I can set something up. It can record, or we can monitor it from a smartphone."

"Thanks. I don't know if he'll be back again after his last exploit. He may be done after beating up the mailbox. Speaking of mailboxes, I bought Mrs. Evans a new one. Have you ever installed one?"

"I can come by tonight to install the camera and the mailbox. It shouldn't take long," he said.

"You're the best! We may not get any more footage of the crazy landscaper, but we'll try. Every time I follow him, he goes to a bar, stops for beer, or goes to the Treasure Chest. He mixes it up every once in a while by checking on a job site. He's sure got a temper. It bothers me that he keeps showing up so close to my house."

"You're the one who gave him the address," Duncan said quietly, staring at his doughnut.

Delanie smirked and picked up the whiteboard marker. She listed all the Tripp sightings beginning with John's truck accident in Amelia County. "I don't think he has anything to do with the Johnny Velvet case, but the first time that I saw him was in Amelia County. He must have been following me back then. But I also saw him at Freeda's and the Treasure Chest. He seems to be quite the regular there. I've caught him following Cooper Richardson too, even after the mayor's death."

"Oh, he's definitely tied to the mayor's case," Duncan said. "And he knows you and what you drive. Whether you want to admit it or not, he's been tailing you for a while. You need either a rental or to switch cars with me."

"I'll get a rental. I don't want to put you out, and I

don't want him following you. I'll hide the Mustang for a few days. I don't think Tripp saw my car when he was at the Evans's house, but he may have tailed me and figured it out. He only talked to me on the phone for a quote on landscaping, but maybe he hasn't linked me with Melanie."

"You don't know that for sure. I think he knows you're connected to Chaz. You need to be careful, Delanie. And we've got to figure out why he's even involved in this at all."

"Do you know what else is odd? I haven't heard back from Richmond PD yet. They acted like a subpoena was imminent. But the article already came out in *Essence Weekly*. I wonder when they'll get around to demanding our Chaz stuff."

"Dunno. Maybe they're chasing other leads. It's already out in the public domain and may not be important any more. I'll make a disc of the video in case you need it."

"Thanks. We should probably add a copy of my report to Chaz too. I have this weird feeling he is telling the truth about all of this. And get this, he thinks Tripp is bad news."

"That's saying something," Duncan said, tearing into his third doughnut. Before he could continue, Delanie's phone buzzed.

"Hello there. How are you? I had a great time at Seasons."

"Hey," said John. "Me too. I'm thinking about taking the afternoon off and going fishing. If I pack a lunch, ya wanna join me?"

"I'd love to… I'm wrapping up things here at work,

but I could be there around noon or so. Does that work for you?"

"Yep. See you then."

"That sounds like fun. Bye," she said as she smiled and disconnected.

Duncan licked the chocolate from his last doughnut off his fingers. He picked up another one from the box, grabbed his laptop, and trotted to his office.

Margaret got up, snorted, and followed Duncan. Delanie wondered what was bothering the two of them.

Her phone dinged, and she read Arthur Thornberg's email that consisted of Thank you. That was the extent of his reply to her report, update, and video of Tyler Peterson. Two of the masks on his condo wall matched the file from the acquisitions director, confirming Thornberg's suspicions about the missing items and his employee.

Delanie pocketed her phone and gathered her things for another trip to John's farm.

Stretched out on a dock in Amelia County, Delanie traded her fishing pole for a mystery novel. John sat nearby, casting into the water every few minutes. It was a perfect Virginia summer afternoon. The bugs buzzed and darted in and out of the water, and there was just enough breeze to rustle the leaves and Delanie's curls.

"Ready for lunch? I packed sandwiches and lemonade in that cooler."

"Sounds good." Delanie reached back and pulled the cooler toward her. "This is a beautiful spot and a gorgeous day."

"Thanks. I've been coming here since I was a kid. This is on the back twenty acres that I inherited from my grandfather. I used to have a tree fort over there," he said, pointing to a copse of three tall oaks. "There's a rope swing over on the other side of the water... I had some great summers here."

"It's idyllic. You need a canoe," she said, looking for traces of the fort in the tree's heavy canopy.

"Not that great for fishing, but a boat would be fun. I always thought I might build a cabin facing the water. It's a nice place to sit and think and to get away from things."

"It is." Delanie unwrapped a turkey and cheese sandwich and took a bite. "If I were you, I'd definitely build a cabin. You'd have your own retreat. You could come out here and never see anyone for days. I could laze on this dock all afternoon."

"I'm thinking about it. It would be nice to have a house on the water," he said, pulling in a fish.

"Have you ever lived on the water before?"

"Nope."

"What was it like in California?"

"I always lived in the city. I had to come back here to breathe." She waited for him to continue, but he turned his attention to his fishing pole. Deciding not to ask any more questions, she picked up her book.

About three hours later, John interrupted Delanie's thoughts with, "Hey, we've got enough for a fish fry. 'Bout ready to head back to the truck?"

Delanie nodded and packed up the picnic remnants. John grabbed the fishing gear and the cooler of fish while she picked up the smaller lunch cooler. Following John back up the path to the dirt road, Delanie snapped a couple of pictures of the pond and the woods with her phone. She even caught one of John leaning against his truck. He had a lost in thought look. *He can't be Johnny Velvet.* She tried to imagine him on stage with throngs of screaming teenagers. Back at the farm, John told Delanie to make herself at home in the kitchen while he cleaned the fish outside near the barn. Through the window, she watched him gut the fish. When he came back, he pulled out the flour and seasonings. He mixed and battered and then dropped the fish in the pan. While he fussed with the frying pan and lid, she boiled water for corn on the cob and put out potato salad as well as fruit salad.

They ate dinner on the deck, and when twilight arrived, he brought out a key lime pie and turned on the strings of twinkle lights that edged the deck and patio area.

"This was as close to perfect as a day can be," she said. "Thank you for sharing it with me. And the meal was fantastic."

"Sounds like you're heading out. You know you don't have to leave." He moved closer and kissed her. One kiss turned into many, and Delanie lost herself in the moment.

She hadn't had romance and fun in a long while. It was nice to have an almost steady boyfriend. She was afraid to bring up the state of their relationship with him. Right now, they both seemed content with the way things were, and she didn't want to ruin it. Though it would have been nice to know if they were exclusive. Plus, she wanted to avoid telling him she was investigating his background for a tell-all writer in California. For now, she forget all about her contract with Tish Taylor.

She pushed thoughts of Johnny Velvet and Tish's book out of her head and enjoyed the John Bailey that was here and now. They left the dirty dishes on the deck.

THIRTY

THE ROOSTER AND other animals in John's menagerie woke Delanie just before dawn with a cacophony of country sounds. His animals could hold their own with any city traffic noise.

Rolling over, she moved closer to John's side of the bed to go back to sleep. She woke when he rolled over and out of bed.

"Sorry," he mumbled. "I didn't mean to wake you. It's seven-thirty, and I'm late with the feeding rounds. I'll be back soon."

She turned over on her side away from the windows. She couldn't fall back to sleep, so she put on her clothes and carried her sandals and purse. She decided to do a little snooping before he came back.

Listening for John, she paused in the hallway and slipped on her shoes. When she didn't hear anything, she tried the doorknob to the first bedroom across the hall from his room. The lock clicked, but it wouldn't open, even with a fair amount of jiggling. She tried the door to the bedroom next door, and it opened with a slight creak. Dozens of boxes stood like stacked sentries around the double canopy bed. More boxes blocked the closet and the bureau.

Delanie listened again for John. When she didn't hear anything, she opened several of the unsealed cartons.

Nothing but books, clothes, and some old toys. Quickly closing the lids, she slipped back out into the hallway.

The locked bedroom door bothered her. She returned to the first door and rummaged through her purse. Finding a bent paperclip in the bottom, she wasted a few minutes trying to pick the lock. When she was about to give up, she heard a pop and a click. Delanie creeped into the locked bedroom and closed the door. Holding her breath, she listened for any sounds of John.

She scanned the room with a blue spread on a twin bed and matching curtains. She focused on an electric guitar propped on a metal stand next to a small amp. It had a yellow lightning bolt on the front. She racked her brain trying to remember if she'd seen that logo before. Delanie snapped a picture of the guitar. It looked modern. *Maybe Duncan can do his magic and locate it in one of The Vibes' pictures.* It's not like Johnny Velvet had a *Lucille* like B.B. King.

The rest of the room was unremarkable. Neat piles of bills and invoices for the farm covered an old wooden desk. She thumbed through them quickly. *That's odd.* The oldest bill dated back to February of this year.

Delanie peeked in a closet and found it jam-packed with clothes and coats on wooden hangers. The room looked like an average bedroom. She wasn't sure why he had to lock the door.

Relocking the door, Delanie slipped back out in the hallway. Before she could cross the hall and rummage through the guest bathroom, she heard the screen door slam.

She found a barefooted John in the kitchen, pulling

out the fixings for an omelet. He hummed as he turned on the gas to heat the frying pan.

Delanie started the coffee and set the table. "I love your house. One day, you'll have to give me a tour of the rest of it."

"Okay. But there's not much to see. It's an old farmhouse, and they're all pretty much alike," he said without turning around from the stove. "The rooms are pretty boxy, but it has a lot of memories. I like it."

They sipped coffee and ate breakfast, mostly in silence. Delanie wished John would say more than just a few words. She seemed to start the majority of their conversations.

"More?" he asked, moving to refill his coffee.

"Oh, no thanks. I'm good. I need to get on the road soon. I have some research to do this afternoon. Can I help you with any of the clean up?"

"No, I got it. If you come back next weekend, I'll give you a tour of the house, and Myrtle will show you around the barn. I'll walk you out."

At her car, he handed her a brown paper bag.

"What's this?"

"Tomatoes and zucchinis from the garden."

Opening the bag, she said, "Thanks. These are huge." She wondered what she was going to do with a big bag of vegetables as she set them on the passenger seat.

John leaned in through the window and kissed her. "Be safe going home," he said as the Mustang roared to life.

"I will. Thanks again." She waved and turned around and headed down the long driveway. She was missing something. It was on the edge of her memory like a dream that she couldn't remember. *Why would John need to lock the door to a bedroom when he lived alone? What did he not want her to see?* She had to figure out what he was hiding. There was something in that bedroom.

THIRTY-ONE

DELANIE STEPPED OUT of the shower, toweled off, and put
on jeans and a T-shirt. She fingered gel through her long
tresses and ran the hairdryer with the diffuser. Stepping over her clothes and sandals from last night, she
grabbed her tennis shoes and headed for the kitchen.
She needed to catch up on email and draft an updated
report for Tish.

Five minutes later, several car horn blasts interrupted
her quiet morning. She didn't hear a fender bender. Looking out the front window, she gasped when she saw
Tripp's truck idling in Mrs. Evans's driveway. He didn't
get out of the truck. Ducking beside her barrel chair, she
peeked around the curtains. It looked like he was making
a call. When he didn't move, Delanie grabbed her collection of cell phones and keys and ducked out the side
entrance. She turned on the disposable phone, and the
voicemail indicator blinked. She climbed in the Mustang
and slumped down behind the wheel.

Delanie was surprised to notice the Evans's new mailbox was in place. Duncan must have come by sometime
yesterday.

The taillights of the truck popped on, and Tripp flew
out of the driveway backwards. He missed going in the
ditch on Delanie's side by inches. Letting him get sev-

eral car lengths ahead, she started the car and idled out of the driveway.

She followed his lane hopping toward downtown Richmond. He surprised her by cutting over three lanes of traffic to the Downtown Expressway. He blew through the E-Z Pass lane without slowing down. Guessing where he was going, Delanie followed him through downtown to the front of the Treasure Chest. Watching him park in the side lot and enter, she pulled in and found an inconspicuous spot where she could spy on the door. He must be going for either a late breakfast or an early lunch. Delanie guessed that the strip show went with either meal. She scooted down in her seat, but more importantly, left the air conditioner running.

After a long wait that included checking her email every thirty seconds, Delanie heard a rap on the window that made her jump. Chiding herself for not paying better attention, she looked up to see Chaz's Marco knocking on the driver's side glass. The large man in black jeans and a dark T-shirt filled up the Mustang's entire side window.

"Hi, Marco," she said, rolling down the window.

"Just checking to see if you're okay. I brought you a drink," he said. He handed her a can through the window.

"Thank you for the Coke. Yes, I'm fine. I'm watching a guy who went in the side entrance about an hour ago."

"You want me to throw him out? He can come out in one piece or several." He smiled, showing a gold tooth.

"No, that's okay. Though it might speed things up. I want to see where he goes from here. But thanks again for the drink."

"No problem. Call me if you need any assistance." Marco disappeared across the lot to the strip club's side entrance.

After texting Duncan about Tripp and his latest antics, she put the phone on the passenger seat and vowed to stay alert. She had been made in the lot by building security. Delanie was usually more careful.

Sipping the soft drink, she watched men go in and out the side door. No females in sight. *The entertainment must use another door.*

She checked her email ten more times and considered calling the bouncer Marco about his offer when she saw Tripp heading for his truck.

Delanie followed three cars behind him down the narrow city streets. He wound through several back streets to Interstate 95. He floored it on the entrance ramp, and Delanie had to amp it up to keep him in sight. His speed stayed consistent at sixty-five miles per hour even though he weaved back and forth across the three lanes. He liked to drive fast and then slam on his brakes.

Tripp did a quick maneuver at the I-95/I-64 interchange, and Delanie had to cut off a silver Accord. She waved a quick apology to the Honda driver's extended horn honking.

Delanie was able to blend in with the early afternoon traffic, and she stayed vigilant, afraid that Tripp could jump off the interstate. They blew through Ashland and by the huge Kings Dominion sign.

Delanie let the gap between her and Tripp get larger and larger. She didn't want him to notice the Mustang in his rearview mirror. He exited the highway and turned abruptly into an entrance for a subdivision called Magnolia Chase. She followed him to a neatly manicured lawn with a large brick two-story house set back several hundred feet from the road. Delanie continued down the street to the next intersection when Tripp pulled into the driveway. From her rearview mirror, she saw him slam the truck door and walk around the side garage to the backyard.

Delanie parked several houses down off the main road where she could still see the truck. She quickly texted Duncan the address of Tripp's latest stop. The McMansions stretched across three- and five-acre lots. She hoped no one would report her strange car parked on the empty street. Most owners either parked in garages, or they weren't home at this time of day.

After no response from Duncan and no sign of Tripp, Delanie locked the Mustang and walked through the neighbor's yard to the opposite side of the house where Tripp had disappeared. She divided her phone, the burner, and her keys between her two front pockets.

Thankful for no dogs or fences, Delanie hid behind a large hydrangea. She peered around the corner of the house.

From the cover of the large bush, she could see an enormous backyard that started at the patio area and continued down a slight slope to the river. A covered dock hugged the water's edge. The backyard looked like a war zone compared to the meticulously cared for front. Piles of dirt and mulch; abandoned lawn tools and a small bulldozer outlined several long ditches and holes. Mud oozed around everything.

Delanie spotted Tripp sitting on a low brick wall with his back to her. He was talking on the phone and waving one arm around like he was swatting bees. Fighting the urge to move closer so she could hear, she stayed put and watched for about ten minutes.

She leaned forward around the corner to see Tripp move to a chaise lounge on the deck, facing the sloping grounds to the river. She strained to hear his heated conversation. His arms flailed from time to time to punctuate whatever he was saying. Delanie watched him in profile for several more minutes.

Delanie darted from the side flowerbed and the hydrangea to a large oak tree directly in front of her and about fifteen feet closer to Tripp's patio. She let out a long sigh when he didn't seem to have seen any movement in his peripheral vision. Hoping to hear something, she flattened herself against the back of the tree trunk. She inched around the right side to sneak a peek. Tripp hadn't moved from his perch. He was tapping furiously on his smartphone.

Delanie stretched and wiggled in place. She tried to ward off the cramps that were starting to tingle in her legs. The pay-as-you-go phone's vibrations echoed in the stillness. Tripp's head whipped around. In what seemed like slow motion, he looked at his phone and then back to the tree.

Delanie bolted into the next door neighbor's backyard. She could hear the slower Tripp lumbering behind her.

Crashing through the hedge and ignoring the tiny cuts, Delanie ran around the corner. The Mustang was about 350 yards away. She poured on speed, hearing only one set of footfalls on the asphalt, she fished out the key fob from her pocket and clicked, jumping into the Mustang and locking the doors. Starting the car, she jammed it in drive and floored the accelerator. An angry and confused Tripp walked toward the street from the neighbor's side yard in one work boot and one socked foot, covered in mud, and carrying his other boot.

After about twenty minutes of checking her rearview mirror constantly, Delanie relaxed. She grabbed the pay-as-you-go phone and flipped through the missed call list. Tripp had left a message. The phone vibrated again with another call from Tripp. She mashed the off button and slammed the phone on the passenger seat. It bounced on the seat and landed on the dark floor mat. With her heart still pounding from the marathon run and the close call, she tried to slow her breathing and come up with a plan. She chided herself for not thinking this through and sacrificing her street address to Tripp.

THIRTY-TWO

ON THE RIDE HOME, Delanie changed lanes every three or four minutes. She exited and reentered the interstate twice in case Tripp was following. She didn't see any sign of the big truck, so she pulled off at Market Square in the Brandermill neighborhood.

She sat in the locked car for what seemed like forever, trying to will her heart and breathing to return to normal rates.

Delanie grabbed her phone and looked for the nearest car rental place. She found the one with the green logo. Ordering a light-colored sedan online, Delanie punched in her credit card number and waited for her confirmation.

Next, she called Duncan. His cell rang and rang. She left a message for him to call her as soon as he could. When she was looking through her emails, Duncan's ringtone chimed.

"Duncan, I'm so glad you called me back. I need a favor. Could you pick me up at the office tonight and drive me in tomorrow morning?"

"I'm fine, thanks for asking. How are you? I'm in the middle of something, but I can be at the office in about an hour or so. What would you do without me? How was Ashland?"

"Since you're busy, I'll fill you in on Tripp and our little visit up north when I see you. Thanks!"

She ended the call and started the Mustang.

When she arrived at Falcon Investigations, she parked in the back by their door and the dumpster and grabbed the burner phone from the floor. Slipping inside, she reset the alarm and moved quickly through the darkened office suite.

Delanie sipped from a bottled water, answered email, and checked Facebook. She heard the door open and close, and she jumped. Duncan and Margaret wandered down the hall to her office.

"Hey, what's going on? Car out back?"

"Yep, by the dumpster." She logged off her laptop. "I've had quite the afternoon. I saw Tripp at the house across the street from me, and I followed him first to the Treasure Chest, and then to the address in Hanover County I texted you. I had the stupid pay-as-you-go phone in my pocket. Tripp called that number and heard the phone buzz. I have never run so far so fast in my life. He saw me and the car when I sped off."

"Okay, so he knows you and the potential client are the same person. He knows your car and where you live."

"It's weird. I know he's followed me, but he's fixated with Melanie not returning his calls. He always calls her Melanie in his voicemail rants."

"Maybe he doesn't know your name?"

"I'm sure he'll return to my house. That's why I want to leave the Mustang out back. Can you take me home and pick me up tomorrow to get the rental?"

"I guess so," Duncan said, shifting his weight from one foot to the other.

"What's the matter? If it's a bother, I can figure something else out."

Duncan hesitated, "Nah. I guess it's okay. I'll pick you up at eight-thirty. Is that too early?"

"No, that's perfect. Thanks, Duncan. I can always count on you."

Before Delanie could continue, he said, "Yep, good ole Duncan. Get your stuff together, and Margaret and I will meet you outside."

Duncan slammed the door on his way out. Delanie wondered what had brought on his sulky mood again. She hoped that her request for rides hadn't caused it. She needed to talk to him, but she couldn't muster the energy right now.

She followed her partner and his faithful dog. Delanie opened the door to Duncan's yellow Camaro, and Margaret gave her a look as she slid in the front seat.

Duncan patted the bulldog's head and said, "It's okay, Baby. You get the backseat to yourself this ride." A few minutes later Duncan parked in Delanie's driveway. Margaret followed them through the kitchen door.

"Can I get you anything?" Delanie asked. She filled a bowl with water and showed it to Margaret, who took a few laps and wandered off toward the living room.

"No, I'm good. On second thought, wanna order a pizza? I have a few cameras I'd like to install to track Tripp if he comes back." Whatever was bothering Duncan earlier seemed to have passed, so she let it go and didn't bring up his moodiness.

"Pepperoni?" Duncan nodded, and she continued. "The cameras are outside only, right? I know it's hypocritical. I don't mind spying for a living. I just don't like cameras in my space."

"Outside only and, yes, it's hypocritical."

He installed the small cameras on some of the window sills or on curtain rods inside the house. "The live feed will be on the website if you want to login and watch. I'll save the feed on one of our servers, and I'll go through it to see if anything interesting pops up," he said.

When the pizza arrived, she asked, "Dunc, what do you want to drink? I have water, ginger ale, Coke, and wine."

"Ginger ale is fine."

They ate in silence until Duncan fed pepperoni to Margaret. She snarfled and chomped loudly, making Delanie and Duncan laugh at her not-so-dainty eating habits.

"Oh. I almost forgot. Did you see the news today?" he asked, wiping the grease off his hands on his jeans.

"No. I was playing hide and seek with Tripp."

"Your museum guy got arrested. I saw a story about Tyler Peterson on Channel 12's website. Good work," he said.

She smiled and patted Margaret on the head.

After cleaning up the remnants of dinner, she said, "It's been a long day. I think I'm about ready to call it a night. Thank you so much for all of your help. I'll see you tomorrow morning. And thanks for putting up the Evans's mailbox."

"Uh, yep," said Duncan. "I think Margaret and I should stay tonight in case he comes back. This guy isn't right."

"You don't have to do that."

"I know, but it will make it easier tomorrow morning. We can sleep on your couch. Margaret and I aren't morning people."

"Tripp is a nut job. But you don't have to babysit me. I'll be okay by myself."

"It'll be easier in the morning," he repeated.

She said, "Okay, I'll get you a blanket and a pillow."

She put Duncan's bedding on the couch and a fleece blanket on the floor for Margaret. Duncan logged back on to his laptop, and Margaret made herself at home.

"Night, guys. If you need something, the bathroom's in the hall, and you know where the kitchen is. Sleep well."

"Will do. I set the cameras to record continuously if they detect motion. We'll see what kind of activity we get. I'll email you a link, so you can see it from your phone or laptop."

Delanie knew that video recording was how they were going to catch Tripp in action, but she was still leery about having cameras in her house, even if they weren't watching her. She wondered if Tripp would show up again on the video feed.

THIRTY-THREE

DUNCAN DROPPED DELANIE off at the car rental store and said he was headed home for a shower.

A few minutes later, she parked the rental in the front row of her office lot and grabbed the acrylic key chain with the rental company's information. Throwing her purse over her shoulder, she looked around for blue trucks. She walked briskly to her front lobby. Making sure to lock the door behind her, Delanie turned on every light through the office suite. She dropped her things on her desk and rifled through the old style paper mail in her inbox.

Waiting for her laptop to boot up, she headed for the kitchen to make coffee. It felt like a morning for something heavily caffeinated. She grabbed the overflowing trash and decided to check on her Mustang. When she opened the door, the carnage in the alley made her drop the bag. She screamed, but nothing came out but a squeak. Trash covered the top and hood of the car, and she smelled gasoline. The headlights, mirrors, side windows, and windshield were shattered. Little bits of glass and trash floated around in a pool of oil. Delanie's stomach dropped. She fought back the tears when she looked at the destruction.

Plopping down on the top of the two wooden steps, she texted Duncan a picture of Black Beauty's demise.

It had to be Tripp. They had never had any issues at the office before. Wiping away a tear, she called her brother's work cell phone.

After two rings, she got a gruff, "Fitzgerald."

"Hi, Steve. I have a problem. Somebody trashed my car."

"Are you okay? Stay inside, and I'll send someone over."

"I'm not at home. I got a rental last night, and I parked the Mustang behind the office. When I checked on it this morning, I found trash all over it. Most of the exterior glass is broken. And there's a huge puddle of oily stuff in the alley."

"I'll call it in, so wait there for the police. I'll swing by in a few. Do you want to tell me what this is really about?"

"I suppose," she said quietly. "There's a guy with a long rap sheet who drives a blue truck, and he keeps showing up in my investigation for Chaz. He's the one I followed that day you and I went downtown. He's involved or knows something about the mayor's murder. And he has a bad temper that he took out on my car."

"And how would you know that he has a temper except for his handiwork on your car?"

"Let's just say that I've witnessed a lot of his antics lately. And obviously, he knows who and where I am."

"Okay. Stay put. We'll talk more when I get there. Go inside and lock the doors until we get there."

The police car pulled in behind the destruction while Delanie was still sitting on the stoop, staring at her car. Fire and hazmat trucks pulled in behind the police cruiser. An officer in green stepped out of his car and put on his Smokey Bear hat. "Ms. Fitzgerald?"

"Yes. I'm Delanie."

"I'm Officer Riley Parker. When did you discover the damage?" While they talked, firefighters created a portable dam to contain the liquids.

"A few minutes ago. I'm a private investigator, and I've been working a case for a client. There's this big, angry guy who keeps popping up at different locations. And I don't think he likes me very much. He's tried to run me off the road once, and he followed me another time. Anyway, as soon as my partner gets here, I'll see what he has on our surveillance cameras. If there's anything, I'll get him to make you a copy. If my hunch is right, we'll see the guy at work."

"Have you ever had vandalism issues here before?" He walked around the car.

"Nope. We've been at this location about three years. We're here at all hours, and we've never had an issue. There's nobody in the suite next to us, and on the other side, there's a consignment shop and a pet shop a little further down. It's a quiet neighborhood. All the neighbors are friendly, and they try to help each other out."

"Then why do you have all the surveillance cameras?"

"Prevention. You know, just in case. Plus, my partner likes to try out new technology. He likes gadgets."

"I'm going to take some pictures and notes. You need to call your insurance company. And, you're going to have to get this oily stuff cleaned up."

Officer Parker took a series of pictures from all sides. As he was poking around the debris, Steve rolled up in his lieutenant's car. He parked behind the fire trucks. Stepping out, he also put on his hat. "Hey, Riley. Hey, D. Looks like you've had better mornings."

She smiled weakly and held the back door for her brother.

By the time Delanie carried two mugs of coffee to her office, Steve had already settled in her chair.

"Hey. That's my seat."

He grinned and moved over to the guest chair. "Okay, so what's going on?"

"I've been following this guy from time to time. He keeps surfacing in Chaz's world, and it overlaps into my investigation."

"Name?"

"Kenneth Albert Payne, III. He goes by Tripp, and he owns Treez Lawn Service and a big, blue Dodge Ram pickup truck. He went to a tony private school with our late mayor's son and Chaz, who says that he's bad news."

"Where have you seen him?" Steve asked, sipping his coffee. "Hmppp. You buy the frou-frou coffee. And if Chaz thinks he's bad news, he must be something."

"Probably. We already know he has a temper. Let's see, the Tripp sightings. I was with a friend in Amelia County a while back, and a blue truck ran us off the country road. The license plate turned out to belong to Tripp, so that's how I figured out who he was. Then I went downtown to talk to the mayor's aide at a club, and Tripp was cruising past the bar. He also showed up at Chaz's place when I was there one day. Oh, and he was the guy in the truck the day you followed me to Richmond PD."

"So, have you met the infamous Tripp?" he asked, putting his coffee mug down on her desk.

"I've talked to him on the phone."

"But he knows who you are?"

"Yes. I think the car is evidence of that." She glared at her older brother.

"So, he knows where you work and what you drive."

"And where I live. I think I got burned in an attempt to get some information out of him. Duncan installed cameras last night around my house. He should be here soon, so we'll check the cameras to see what they picked up."

"Okay," said Steve, inhaling deeply. He let it out slowly and continued, "So, what else are you not telling me."

"Why do you ask that?"

"Because it's what you do. Spill the rest of it, or I can't help you."

Before she could answer, her phone vibrated. Duncan texted that he was in the car in the front lot with a disc. "Hold on." She replied to Duncan and said, "Duncan's got the footage. Wait here and I'll go get it."

"I'm beginning to think that your partner is really your imaginary friend. You didn't make him up, did you?"

"No, smarty pants. Duncan's a real guy. You met him a couple of times when I was in college. He prefers hanging out with his dog and his computers." She darted out the suite's front door. She didn't mention that Duncan had creative ways of getting information. Everyone else called it hacking. Duncan didn't like being around law enforcement if he could help it. He didn't use his abilities to scam anyone, but he still stretched laws in a way that probably wasn't acceptable in Steve's circles.

When she returned, Delanie put the disc in her lap-top and clicked on the viewer. After a few seconds of nothing but the Mustang and the back of the office, a dark truck appeared in part of the frame. A large guy in jeans and a dark shirt with a ball cap pulled low walked into the frame and crawled under the car. He slid out quickly and disappeared off camera. Then something started oozing out of the car and puddling in the alley. A few seconds later, he returned with a baseball bat and went to town. The timestamp read 3:15 AM. After his destructive dance, he pulled two plastic garbage bags out of the back of his truck. He sliced the bottom of each with a large knife and spread the contents on the car. Then he left the bags on the car.

"That Tripp?" Steve asked.

"Yep. I'm pretty sure it is. That's his blue Dodge. You can see part of the plate with his TREEZ advertising on it."

"Okay, let me have that. I'll add my notes to the complaint against Tripp Payne, and Officer Parker'll email you a copy to review and sign. You need to call your insurance company and somebody to clean up the gasoline. And I still want the rest of the story. I'll call you later today. If you're going to stay at your place, I want to come by and check it out."

"Okay. I haven't thought that far. If I don't stay there, I'll let you know. Thanks for your help."

After Steve and the other officer left, Delanie locked the back door and then checked the locks at the front of the office. She left the lights on in the lobby and hallway. After rummaging through her wallet for her insurance information, she texted Duncan that she was alone, and it was safe to return to the office.

SETTLING ON HER couch with a mug of hot tea, Delanie was ready to forget about Tripp and her car with mind-numbing TV when a knock on the door interrupted. Glancing at her laptop on the coffee table to check the camera feed, she was relieved to see Steve on the front porch.

"Come on in," she said, unlocking the front door.

"You didn't check before you opened it," he said, stepping into her cozy living room.

"Laptop. I could see you on camera."

"Okay, good." He walked around the living room, shaking locked windows and looking at the cameras. "You need to go down to the courthouse tomorrow and take out a restraining order against Tripp."

"How much good is that going to do? He's not one to follow the rules."

"It will at least get the process started and the docu-mentation on record. He's a loose cannon. He's got a record a mile long, and he's known to have anger man-agement issues." He walked through the kitchen and checked the back door. "I'd feel better if you stayed with someone for a few days." His voice came to her from somewhere in the back of the house. "We're looking for him, but he's not at his usual haunts."

When Steve returned to the living room after check-ing the upstairs, she said, "I appreciate the concern, but I'm okay here. I have a gun and the cameras. I parked the rental car in the back, and I'll be careful. I'm not going to live in fear of some psycho-bully. I'm one of the good guys. And he doesn't get to win."

"Okay, I knew you were going to be stubborn. You have to promise me that you'll call me if you so much as think he's nearby."

"I can do that, but I'm guessing he's hiding until he thinks the pressure's off. He won't show up around here any time soon. I think he took his fury out on my car. He's probably tied one on, and now he's sleeping it off somewhere."

"Speaking of your Mustang, what happened after I left?"

"The insurance company is taking care of it. We'll see how long a process this turns out to be," she said, changing the television station. "I hope she's the same after they fix her. I couldn't believe what I saw yesterday. That guy is an idiot."

"He's definitely a nut job. We're looking for him all over Central Virginia, so he should feel the pressure soon. I'll let you know when we get him." He headed to the door. "Call me if you need me."

"Thanks, Steve. And hang on to him when you get him. He's guilty of more than just destroying a mailbox and my car."

"Mailbox?"

"It's a long story. I'll fill you in later."

Steve rolled his eyes and blocked the door as she tried to shut it behind him. "What mailbox?"

"The mailbox for the house across the street. When I looked out the window the other day, it was in several pieces."

"Why do you think he did it? It could be kids in the neighborhood."

"He's been by several times."

"Delanie—"

"Thanks for all of your help. I promise I'll be vigilant."

Delanie heard Steve sigh as she shut and locked the front door.

On a whim, she dialed Marco. After four rings, she left him a message to call her and the police if Tripp showed up again at Chaz's club. She texted him a photo for good measure. Tripp was guilty of more than property damage. She had to figure out a way to link him conclusively to the mayor's murder.

THIRTY-FOUR

DELANIE TOSSED AND turned for hours and chided herself for being silly. *Tripp's not going to get the best of me.* He messed up her car and her plans, but she wasn't going to be afraid to sleep in her own house.

After breakfast and a shower, Delanie forced herself to finish the report for Tish Taylor. Avoiding the distraction of social media, she read her update and made a few changes. Her opinion for Tish and Tod was that John Bailey of Amelia County wasn't Johnny Velvet of The Vibes. She cited a string of reasons, but they looked weak when she reread them. She closed with the information that the DNA testing was ongoing, and it could be weeks or even months before she received the results. She said that she would update them again once she had the report from the lab. She suppressed guilty feelings about not being professional. She already knew what the results would be on Emily's sample and Duncan's toothbrush. She attached her report with what she thought was her final expense sheet, and she pressed send before she could change her mind and rewrite the report. She had never lied about an investigation before.

A flicker on the laptop camera window distracted her. She paused and let out a breath when she realized that the truck across the street was a mailman on his rounds. She was annoyed at herself for being jumpy.

Delanie shifted her worry about Tripp to her future business. Concerned that the pipeline was empty, she sent emails to two insurance company contacts to see if they had anything they could funnel her way in the near future.

Restless, Delanie was pondering what to do for the rest of the afternoon when she was interrupted by banging on the door.

Delanie checked the laptop and went to the living room to let Duncan in. He and Margaret came bearing lunch and a stack of folders.

"Hey, Dunc. Hey, Margaret. What's up?"

"We brought food and some ideas."

"Then you're welcome to come on in. I've been working in the kitchen."

After spreading out roast beef sandwiches and potato cakes, Duncan pulled some meat out for Margaret, who inhaled it without savoring the slow roasted taste.

"So, whatcha got?" Delanie asked between bites of sandwich and sips of iced tea.

"The car's destruction bothered me," Duncan said.

"It bothered me too," she said with a smirk.

"Not yours. I'm sorry about that, but I was thinking about Johnny Velvet's. How many times have we seen that video Tod sent?"

"I dunno. Ten or twelve times."

"What's wrong with it?" he probed, setting up his laptop on her kitchen table.

"It's old. It's grainy. It's kind of dark in parts."

"Okay, but there's a lot more wrong with it. Watch this." He clicked on a link, and they watched a Trans

Am catch fire and explode near a barn. It only took seconds for the entire area to be engulfed in a fireball.

"I give up. It looks similar to Johnny Velvet's accident except for the bridge and the water."

"That's right. Johnny Velvet's car hit a cement pylon and flipped off a bridge into the reservoir. A huge fireball materialized before the car dropped into the water. And only one passenger had time to escape. He went off the road on the passenger side. Yet, Jake Kowalski, the passenger, was able to escape while Johnny Velvet, the driver, couldn't."

"Jake might have been ejected," Delanie said.

"Possibly, but it doesn't matter. In this stunt video, the car jumped a ditch and hit a barn head on. Then it blew up the same way that Johnny Velvet's did." Duncan took a breath and continued. "Wait for it. Here's the big reveal. The stunt team on the Trans Am video was led by Kevin Kowalski, Jake's brother."

Her stomach did a flip-flop. It definitely looked like the same kind of accident. "Then it stands to reason that the same team planned Johnny Velvet's accident," she replied.

"I did some research. And thanks to the guys at *Mythbusters* who did an episode on car explosions, I realized what bothered me most about the video."

"And that was?"

"The fact that someone taped it at all is troublesome. People didn't walk around with cell phones back then. Someone with a heavy video recorder had to be on or near that bridge at twilight at the exact time of the accident. It felt like a setup. I looked to see if anyone else had questioned it, but I couldn't find anything. Then I started looking at the explosion, over and over and over. Cars do blow up, but it's usually when the gas tank is hit dead on or is ignited in some way." Delanie nodded as Duncan continued. "You saw the video. He hit a cement bridge head on. The gas tank is in the back. The worst that could have happened was that the radiator exploded. It would have done a lot of damage to the car, but it wouldn't have created an inferno. I even looked at film from the '70s when Pintos and other dangerous cars blew up. They exploded and created massive fireballs because their fuel systems were faulty. John's car was brand new at the time of the accident. And the accident happened at the end of autumn in 1988. I checked. That car hasn't had recalls or issues with the fuel systems."

"And how did it launch off the bridge?"

"I think it was a fake. From the way it was videoed, it looks movieish," he said, reaching for his drink. "He would have had to have a ramp or something."

"So, you're saying the accident was a big setup. It was staged all along," Delanie said.

"Yes," Duncan said, taking a bite of his sandwich.

"That fits," Delanie said. "That's why there was no body, and the police reports are sketchy. I wonder if somebody paid someone off. We can't be the first people to dig into this after all these years, can we?"

"It was all Hollywood flash," Duncan said. "I'm surprised that somebody hasn't questioned the video sooner. To get an explosion like that you would have to tamper with the fuel line, or you have to set up an explosion. It's not probable with a normal car accident. Most head-on collisions do not cause fireballs. So, the rumors that Tish and Tod had heard about sabotage may have had a little truth to them."

"Okay, so you're saying the car was engineered to explode," Delanie said.

"Yes, the car was rigged, plain and simple," Duncan said. "And I'm surmising that Johnny probably didn't die in that car accident. But I have no real proof. The video stops and picks up again with Jake in the street. It wasn't one continuous scene. We need to keep looking into the other surviving band members. I can't believe they could keep a secret this long. I also couldn't find any record of the car in any of the police reports. I know stuff gets lost, especially before the files were electronic. But nobody had any details on the investigation or what happened to the car. I couldn't find anything about it being pulled out of the water. There wasn't the slightest report anywhere. It's odd that the wreck wouldn't be picked over and photographed after a celebrity's death. Makes me think that someone paid someone to *lose* the records."

"I can buy your car fire theory. But if it was a cover up so that Johnny Velvet could live a quiet life somewhere else, why not contact his daughter?" Delanie asked. "John Bailey acts like family is important to him. But on the other hand, it doesn't seem probable that all his friends and bandmates could keep a secret for that long. Somebody would leak this story. Jake Kowalski couldn't keep his mouth shut if his life depended on it, but he didn't waver from the story. Maybe he's a better actor than I gave him credit for. And could you walk away from that type of lifestyle? I've been in John's farmhouse. There's no trace of anything that even remotely resembles rich rock star. He drove an ancient truck until he was forced to buy a new one. Plus, if it were a fake accident, Jake would have had some inside knowledge," she said, taking a bite of her potato cake.

"Who said he hasn't had any contact? Or maybe he's not social. You said that John was quiet. He's got a new life, and he likes it. Maybe it was time to just get out," Duncan said.

"Could it be that simple? John does seem to be an uncomplicated guy. When he's talking, I try to picture him as Johnny Velvet, but I can't. He's always John Bailey in jeans and a flannel shirt. He wears Old Spice. Not much seems to bother him, and he definitely operates on his own timetable. There are no clues that he's anything other than what he appears to be. He never hums old '80s songs or hints that he has any musical abilities. All I found was that guitar in his guest bedroom," she said. "Did that turn up anything, Dunc?"

"I looked through old videos and pictures. I checked for photos of one like it, and I didn't see any lightning bolt images on any of The Vibes' stuff. It might just be a guitar from his high school days. Or it may be one that he likes. The next time you're there, you should ask him to play it."

"Can't, because he doesn't know that I saw it."

"Well, the accident was a fake. That I'm sure of," Duncan said. "They just didn't think through the scenario. It would have been better if Jake, the survivor, had been driving. I'm still surprised that no one else has dug into this. The only 'after the accident' information that I could find were claims of Johnny Velvet sightings in different cities."

"Why? Why didn't anyone pursue this?" Delanie said exasperated. "There was no insurance and no dead body. The band members didn't leak the secret. Think about it, the public is still fascinated with James Dean's death. Why isn't there the same fascination about Johnny Velvet's death? We've got to follow the money. It was a long time ago. And the agent, Bob Groome, is dead. What can you do about looking at Johnny Velvet's money? Can you use your Internet magic to see what's still there? I suspect some payoffs."

"I'll see what I can find. But a lot of time has passed."

"If it's out there, I know you'll be able to find it."

"Hey," Duncan interrupted. "You know that night at Freeda's. You said that you owed me a favor. I know what you can do."

"What are you talking about?"

"You said you owed me for dragging me out to that bar. I thought of something that you can do for me. You can go with me tonight to an event."

"Like a date?"

"No. It's RVACon. It's a comic book and pop culture conference, and there's a contest tonight."

She sighed and hoped he didn't hear. "Okay, Duncan. If it'll make you happy, I'll go. What do I have to do?"

"It's at the Convention Center downtown, and I already have tickets. Be there by six, dressed and ready to go."

"Against my better judgment, what does 'dressed and ready to go' mean?"

"Your costume's in the car. I'll go get it. My World of Warcraft team is doing a themed thing. It'll be fun. And we need a female to make it over the top."

Delanie sighed again, and this time, she didn't care if he heard.

When Duncan returned from his car, he handed her a purple and black outfit and a pair of platform boots. "Go try it on."

Returning from the bathroom after transforming into Batgirl, Delanie said, "It's scary that you know my sizes."

"You look great! And you can keep it if you want to afterwards. See you downtown at six. Meet me out front."

Interrupted by her phone's text chime, she slid her finger across the screen. John had sent her a message about the upcoming rodeo. She quickly texted back that eleven o'clock tomorrow at his place would be great.

THIRTY-FIVE

BATGIRL DROVE DOWNTOWN to the convention center. She was surprised at what Duncan spent money on. This wasn't a plastic Halloween costume. It was Spandex, and it looked theatre quality.

Delanie felt silly driving to Richmond as the purple superhero. She got some interesting honks and waves from the other drivers. The guy in the lane next to her at the tollbooth took her picture.

After leaving her car in the parking deck, she found a short Batman at the front entrance in a full rubber suit waving his arms like a windmill.

"Hey," he said when she got closer. "Hurry up."

"I'm here, and I'm dressed."

"You look good, but Batgirl didn't carry a purse."

"This one does. I'm not walking back to the car; besides, we don't have time. Come on."

"Okay, but it's not authentic," he muttered, following behind her to the main ballroom. "We just better not lose because of it. Oh, I didn't warn you. Most of the people here in costumes are amateurs, but there are some that you need to be aware of."

"Like who?"

"When people like us dress up, it's called cosplay. Then there's cross play, and it's when guys dress as girls and vice versa. Most people go to be seen and photographed, but there's an etiquette to follow if people want to take your picture. There are some other kinky folks in costume, usually the furry ones. Hopefully, you won't get propositioned."

Delanie rolled her eyes. "I think I can take care of myself." She followed Duncan into a ballroom. "Where are we supposed to be?"

"Over there." He pointed with the rubber glove at a table near the stage. A Joker, Two-face, and Riddler waited for them.

"Hey, guys," Duncan said. "This is my partner, Delanie. I think we're ready."

"This is so awesome," the Riddler said. "We've never had a Batgirl before. This could be our year to nail the prize. None of the other Justice League teams have any female characters."

"Delanie, this is Nadir as the Joker. Li is the Riddler, and Douglas is Two-face."

"Hi, guys. What, no Robin?"

"No," Nadir said. "We thought you'd make a better Batgirl than Robin."

"I was going to dress up Margaret, but the center has pet rules. Plus, you have long, red hair like Yvonne Craig in the wig from the television series. We thought you'd be perfect. And I didn't think you'd have liked any of the Catwoman costumes," Duncan interjected.

Delanie smiled at her tablemates.

The guys resumed their conversation about which Catwoman was the best. It seemed to be a tie between Julie Newmar and Eartha Kitt. She tuned out their discussion.

Delanie enjoyed looking at all the costumes. She saw

every facet of pop culture imaginable that ranged from superheroes to *Star Wars* characters. She had no idea what some of the creatures were.

An emcee interrupted her scan of the crowd when he thunked a microphone and started calling each group's name for them to parade across the stage.

"And next we have another Batman troupe, Gotham's Geeks," the announcer said.

"That's us," Nadir yelled, jumping to his feet and almost tipping over the chair.

"Leave your purse here," Duncan said. "Okay, show time. Make it good, guys! This is for all the marbles."

Delanie shoved her purse under the table and wound the strap around one of the chair legs. She hoped that it would be here when she returned. She hid her keys and phone in her bat utility belt.

The fabulous five walked across the stage and strutted and posed. The Joker and the Riddler got laughs when they did an impromptu dance.

On a whim, Delanie decided to spice it up. She walked around and teased the villains and gave Batman a sexy hug to a standing ovation. Chaz would be proud of her.

The emcee narrowed down the list of the best groups, and Gotham's Geeks were in the top three. For the last round in front of the crowd, the team upped the ante and poured on the antics. Delanie was surprised at the applause.

The Gotham Geeks won, and Duncan couldn't contain himself.

After all of the jumping and hugging, they made their way to the table with first prize, a five-hundred dollar gift card for the convention's market area.

"So, what's next?" she asked as she plopped in the chair to catch her breath.

"Oh, bragging rights for the rest of the conference. And we're going to spend our winnings. And there's a lot more to see. Plus, there's some paranormal investigators and some guys from Area 51 that I want to hear later."

"Okay, but I think I'm going to take off if you don't need me anymore."

Duncan hesitated and then said, "Uhhh, okay. I guess we're done here. Thanks for helping us. But don'tcha want to spend your part of the take? There are some interesting things in the market place. They even have girl stuff like jewelry."

"Oh, you guys deserve the prize money. I had fun. Thanks for the costume."

A short, bespectacled Hermione Granger interrupted when she grabbed Duncan's arm. "Congratulations. You guys look great together. You outdid yourselves with the costumes. Y'all were the best Justice League here." She pushed her glasses up on her nose with her index finger.

"Uh, thanks," Duncan stammered.

Delanie smiled and waved to the Gotham Geeks. She heard the young woman, who was standing very close to Duncan say, "Hi, I'm Evie Hachey."

"Bye," the rest of villains said in unison, and Douglas waved. The short Batman and Evie continued their conversation, ignoring everyone around them.

Delanie grabbed her bag and headed for the restroom. This was her first Comicon, complete with costume. It wasn't how she planned to spend her evening, but it was different. Maybe she'd reprise the role for Halloween. And maybe Duncan had met a new friend.

On her way through the main doors, Delanie caught her breath. Ahead of her, she spotted John Bailey leaning on the information desk.

Taking the papers that he was handed, John turned and walked toward the market place. Delanie tailed him from a few feet back. She was shocked to see him there. He never even hinted at liking anything except his farm and his truck, but she did find some action figures in one of his boxes.

She pretended to look at the wares of the tables she passed. John stopped at several booths and looked at comic books. He entered a booth where collectibles hung from every available space. She eavesdropped on his back and forth banter with the clerk. John finally purchased two Star Wars action figures and a set of KISS dolls.

Delanie walked past him and said, "Nice action figures," as she tried to disguise her voice.

He smiled and said, "For my collection. Cool costume."

"Thanks. Where's yours?"

"I'm not a diehard fan. I'm just a collector."

"You collect rock star memorabilia?" Batgirl asked.

"Sometimes. Usually stuff from the seventies and eighties."

"What's your favorite?"

John paused. "Probably KISS."

Delanie was hoping for some new information. "You look familiar," she prodded. "You famous?"

"Nah," he said. "People always think I look like somebody. I'm here people watching."

"Well, enjoy. There's lots to see." She turned and headed to the exit.

John walked toward the concession stand and the breakout rooms. She wondered what presentation got his attention. She texted Duncan to be on the lookout for John.

She kicked herself for missing the opportunity to see if he would have taken the phone number of the mysterious superhero in a purple outfit. But then she smiled. Her farm guy liked comic books and action figures. Maybe she would have an occasion to reuse the Batgirl costume.

DELANIE THREW THE deadbolt on her front door and wandered to the kitchen to find a snack. There still wasn't anything appealing in the refrigerator, so she ordered Chinese takeout.

She didn't have any plans, so she changed into her pajamas and settled on her bed with her takeout and laptop, sorting through all of her John Bailey notes. She put her recent photos at the lake next to some of Johnny Velvet from the Internet. Besides the height and the eye color, she didn't see any other obvious resemblance. It was hard to imagine John Bailey from Amelia County giving up all claims to his daughter. Something didn't feel right. But she found out something new about him today, so maybe there was more to this guy. Delanie drifted off to sleep thinking about John Bailey and Johnny Velvet of The Vibes.

She heard a loud clunk and several quieter thunks. She woke up to a dark room, illuminated by the blue light on her laptop. Delanie listened, trying to decide whether the noise came from inside of the house. She heard some scraping, so she opened Duncan's application and checked the cameras. A figure in a dark hoodie strode down her driveway with a shovel and what looked like a bag. He disappeared around the corner before she could get to the front window. The cameras didn't catch any parked vehicles.

Ducking down to watch for his return, she called Steve on his cell phone.

"Hey, I'm sorry to wake you, but I've got a problem," she said.

"I was awake. What's up?" He sounded slightly groggy.

"I woke up to a noise. I saw a guy in dark clothes walking down my driveway with a shovel. I think he's gone, but I couldn't tell from the cameras what he was doing."

"Okay, stay put. I'll send a car by, and I'll be there in about a half hour. Don't go near the door until you're sure that it's the officer."

"Thanks. You're great," she said. "I love you."

"Love you too. See you in a few," he said, clicking off.

Delanie sat with her back to the door until she heard a car pull into the gravel. A quick check confirmed a Chesterfield County cruiser parked in her driveway.

A few minutes later, an officer knocked on the door.

"Delanie Fitzgerald?" she said. "I'm Officer Christine Tate." She flashed an identification card and badge.

"Yes, please come in."

"What's this?" the officer asked, looking at something on Delanie's porch.

Delanie opened the door and groaned when she saw the dead possum on the tiny landing. It was stretched out like it was lying in a bear rug pose. A large kitchen knife with a wooden handle stuck out of its neck, and fluids oozed out and puddled on her porch.

"Ewwww. I guess my intruder left this mess. Please come in if you can step over it." She held the door for the young officer.

Steve pulled in the driveway beside the cruiser as Officer Tate finished her interview. She took several pictures of the mutilated marsupial. The officer bagged the knife, and Steve asked Delanie for a shovel. He buried the possum in the backyard behind the flower bed.

"What's going on?" he asked after Officer Tate backed out of the driveway.

"I couldn't identify my night visitor on the video stream. He was wearing dark clothes. I saw him walking down the driveway. I didn't see or hear a car or a truck. But I have a hunch it's Tripp."

"I want you to be very careful. Do you want to stay with us?"

"No, I'm a big girl. I'm not letting some idiot chase me out of my own house. I promise that I'll call again if I have any more problems. I think he's gone for the night. He wanted to scare me, or it's some kind of weird prank. Any other reports of animal mutilations lately?"

"Not around here. It's been a while. We had a goat voodoo thing going on last summer near Route One.

"I don't think it's a random prank, and it didn't look like an animal sacrifice. I'm pretty sure that I know who left me this present. Thanks for coming out at oh-dark-thirty. And for taking care of the possum for me."

"No problem. But you're going to want to bleach that porch tomorrow. Hey, do me a favor."

"What?"

"Find some normal clients."

"Tripp isn't my client. And my job's fun most days. Don't forget that I worry about you too. You don't exactly deal with choirboys."

He nodded and patted Delanie on the top of her head.

She locked the deadbolt in place behind him. Relieved that Steve didn't ask about the restraining order that she hadn't filed, Delanie sighed and leaned her back on the door. She felt that pressing charges for the car damages was enough. A restraining order wouldn't stop Tripp.

Too keyed up to sleep, she pored over the video to see if her night visitor looked anything like Tripp. She couldn't distinguish much between the darkness and the guy's shrouded garb. All she saw was the back of a figure walking down the driveway.

She texted Duncan the timestamp and camera number with hopes that he could do something to the resolution to confirm that it was Tripp. Meanwhile, she would be hypervigilant in case her night visitor returned.

THIRTY-SIX

JOHN PARKED HIS truck in the field where the teenager in an orange vest pointed. Delanie jumped out before John could come around and open her door. Dodging the muddy spots, they hiked about a hundred yards through a field to get to the rodeo.

They stepped up to the barrel where a deputy checked Delanie's purse and waved them through. Brightly colored flags and balloons danced in the breeze. Vendor booths and small rides encircled the stadium.

"Hungry?"

"I can always be hungry for fair food. But no fried pickles," she said. She held his hand and looked at the "as seen on TV" booths.

They settled for hot dogs and cheese fries at a wooden picnic table near one of the barns.

Delanie finished her hot dog in a few bites and balled up the wrapper. She pushed the cheese fries closer to John.

"You downed that in record time. Oh, I forgot you're a city girl. Don't like having lunch near the earthy barn smells?"

"I'm a mall girl. And I'm not used to critters except Margaret, my friend's English bulldog. She smells sometimes, but not this bad." Delanie wrinkled her nose.

After clearing their trash, John led the way through

the vendors to the stadium's entrance. "Let's go stake out some seats. It doesn't start until later, but we should be able to get a good view." Delanie nodded.

She followed him through the tunnel area under the stands and up the wooden bleachers to seats about ten rows up behind the stalls. They sat quietly looking at the empty arena. A few people trickled in and found seats. Guys dressed like cowboys led animals to the pens.

"I need to find the little cowgirls' room. I'll be back in a minute. Need anything while I'm up?"

"Nah. I'll just wait here in the sunshine." John pulled down the brim of his Washington Nationals ball cap to cover his eyes. He kicked back and closed his eyes.

Walking through the throngs of rodeo patrons, Delanie felt someone bump into her and shake her shoulder. She jumped and stiffened. With her heart pounding, she turned and saw a tall man in jeans and a T-shirt with an even taller woman. He said, "Hey, Delanie, is that you?"

She didn't recognize the guy or the blond in hot pink shorts and a tank top. "Delanie, it's me, Jarrod, Jarrod Rawlings."

"Oh, hi, Jarrod," she replied, searching her brain for where she remembered him from. He looked slightly familiar, but she couldn't place the face.

"How are you? I haven't seen you since Paisley's party last summer," Rawlings said. "You here for the rodeo?"

Captain Obvious. It's that Jarrod. He was dating Paisley last summer, and he had a cabin on the river where they spent the fourth of July. But he couldn't hold Paisley's attention for more than a couple of months.

"It's good to see you," Jarrod. "And yes, it's my first rodeo."

"Mine too," squeaked his companion.

"Well, we should be going. It was good to see you," Jarrod said.

"You too. I'll tell Paisley I ran into you. Have fun!" On her way to the restroom, Delanie heard a "Who's Paisley?"

She chided herself for being so jumpy. She took a deep breath to get rid of the nervousness. The whole Chaz and Tripp thing was on her mind too much lately.

She texted Paisley that she ran into Jarrod and his new girlfriend. Pictures? was the only response she received from her friend.

Retracing her steps from the bathroom, Delanie noticed that the crowd had thinned quite a bit. She followed the graveled walkway around and stopped suddenly. She spotted Tripp Payne leaning against a wooden light pole and talking on his cell phone.

Ducking behind a lemonade booth, Delanie peeked around the corner to see if he had spotted her. She watched while he waved his arms around and carried on a heated conversation. She grabbed her phone and called Steve. When she got his voicemail, "Hey, Steve, it's me. John Bailey and I are at the rodeo at the Powhatan Fairgrounds. I came out of the bathroom and saw Tripp Payne here. Call or text me when you can."

Tripp continued to talk loudly and wave his free arm around. He finally disconnected and looked around at the crowd and walked away.

Not wanting to lose Tripp, she tried to keep him in her line of sight but leave enough space so he wouldn't notice her. At least when Steve called back, she'd know where Tripp was.

Wishing she had John's ball cap, she scrunched down slightly. Putting her head through the strap of her purse, she hunched over slightly. She hoped Tripp didn't turn around.

Walking to the side entrance, Tripp exited through the unmanned gates. Delanie followed behind him. About forty tractor-trailers, parked at all angles, covered the field.

The trucks were Delanie's only cover. She followed Tripp down a makeshift row. Signaling to someone inside of a cab, Tripp swung open the passenger door and climbed in. The rig was parked about twenty-five feet away from Delanie's hiding place. Tinted windows prevented Delanie from seeing what Tripp and his friend were doing.

The truck beside her offered the best view for snooping. She picked her way around the driver's side through a squishy mess of rocks and mud puddles. She kept poking her head around the truck to see if Tripp had moved. Afraid he would notice the movement, she grabbed a metal bar and swung herself up to the outside small space between the cab and the trailer.

Pressed against the back of the truck in the three feet of space, Delanie peered through the cab, but it was too dark to see anything. She stepped across the metal landing and leaned over and squatted on the passenger side to watch for Tripp's exit.

Delanie's legs started to tingle. She was almost ready to give up when she heard someone whistling. She pressed herself up against the cab below the window in hopes that she was out of sight of whoever was approaching. The whistler neared, and she heard footsteps. Then the cab door opened and slammed. The diesel engine sputtered, and the engine rumbled. Delanie froze for a few seconds. At the moment she moved over to the edge to jump off the back, the truck jerked when the driver put it in gear.

The truck rolled through the field toward the road. She moved to the driver's side. She closed her eyes, put her head down, and jumped before the truck picked up any more speed.

Landing in the dirt and grass, Delanie rolled over several times before she came to a hard stop on her arm. Dirt and dust flew from the truck that was getting smaller and smaller.

She stood up slowly and didn't care if Tripp saw her. Nothing ached too badly except her pride. Delanie stepped behind another tractor-trailer to catch her breath and check for bruises. Her shirt and jeans were covered in dirt and damp mud, and she probably had stuff in her hair too. Brushing off as much as she could, Delanie wondered how she would explain her disheveled appearance to John. At least she still had her purse.

Delanie re-entered the fairgrounds and returned to the restroom. When she walked in, two women at the sink stopped talking to stare at her. When she gawked back, the women quickly exited. She wasn't in the mood to make small talk with strangers.

Her reflection shocked her. It looked like she had been wrestling with a pig, and the pig had won. Delanie left the restroom and waded through the crowd to the amphitheater. She hoped John wouldn't think she had abandoned him. She pulled out her phone, but decided against texting John.

When she rounded the first turn, someone grabbed her bruised shoulder and dragged her in a different direction. Delanie's blood ran cold when she felt metal push against her shirt. This wasn't a friendly hello tap from an acquaintance or a bump from someone in the crowd. The end of a barrel hit the bone in her spine and caused her to wince.

Before she could react to the gun, a man leaned in and whispered in her ear. "Just act natural. Keep walking." She recognized the voice from all the messages left for Melanie. She slid her phone in her front pocket.

Tripp poked her again in the back with the gun. His hot breath smelled of stale cigarettes and whiskey. He shoved her toward the barns to the right. He was standing so close that they probably looked like they were a couple. Shivering at the thought, Delanie took a deep breath and tried to slow her heart rate. She was sure Tripp could hear the pounding.

When she didn't move, he gave her a push and stuck the gun harder into her spine. Delanie began walking. There wasn't another soul anywhere in their path.

THIRTY-SEVEN

TRIPP SHOVED DELANIE AGAIN, this time in the direction of the barn farthest from the amphitheater. The green and white door was ajar, and Delanie didn't see anyone that she could signal about her plight.

Guiding her forcibly forward, Tripp leaned on her several times, once bumping her hard enough to make her stumble. Inside the barn, she blinked a couple of times to adjust to the cooler, darkened interior. The smell of hay and animals made her nose itch. Tripp huffed and puffed and wheezed as he prodded her with the gun toward the back of the barn that housed a few horses, a donkey, and a buffalo that snorted at their entrance.

"Where are we going?" she hissed.

"Shut up, bitch, and keep moving. You'll find out soon enough."

Before she could say anything else, Tripp stopped near the back of the darkest stall.

He grabbed her purse strap and pushed her into the hay. Landing face first, the strap broke, and the purse landed close to Tripp. When she tried to scoot away, he stomped his steel-toed work boot on the back of her right leg. She screamed, the pain bouncing off her spine and spinning around her head. She gulped several deep breaths to keep from blacking out.

Before she could get away, he stomped again on her ankle. Tripp smacked at her with the gun, but Delanie scooted into the back corner on top of a pile of fresh hay. He leaned over and kicked the purse out of her reach. Stumbling, Tripp steadied himself by holding onto the wooden post at the front of the stall. Delanie touched something hard and cold.

She dug down further. It was a pitchfork. She kept her hand on the base of the handle. She swallowed hard to get control of her nerves and to suppress the throbbing in her leg and ankle.

"You think you're so smart, but I figured it out," Tripp slurred, obviously drunk. "You've been sticking your nose in my business for too long now. You cost me money. I thought you were a paying job, and you tricked me into coming out to the boonies. Then I realized it was you. You're always snooping. And you think you're so hot, but you're not. I figured out what you're about. You should have backed off and minded your own business. You had plenty of warnings." He sprayed spit as he talked.

"I don't know what you're talking about," she said. "I think you have the wrong person."

"Oh, sister, I've got the right person. You're the one with the black Mustang, or should I say were. You needed to be taught a lesson. Why couldn't you just leave things alone? You were going to ruin everything for Patrick. It was all taken care of, and it's none of your business. You should have stayed in Podunk and stopped nosing around." Tripp wobbled, still unsteady on his feet.

"I have no idea who you are," Delanie said in her softest voice. She tried to make herself smaller in the corner. When she moved, her leg hurt.

"That stupid mayor and his boyfriend were ruining things for the Hunters," Tripp said. "Somebody had to do something for Mrs. Hunter. Her husband had a thing on the side with another guy, younger than Patrick. It would have killed her." Tripp's voice got louder and more aggressive, waving his arms and the gun around as he talked.

Tripp stopped for a moment. Delanie noticed that his eyes flitted around the barn, never stopping to focus on any one thing.

"All I was doing was helping Patrick protect his mother and sister. It would have died down, but you kept stirring things up. You should have left things alone. And so what if everyone wanted to blame the slimy strip club owner. Good riddance. That got rid of two blights on society. And when I get rid of you, it'll be over, and things will go back to normal. Especially if the mayor's friend knows what's good for him. He should be quiet and go away. Or I can make him go away." Tripp paused, breathing heavily. "And who's going to miss you? You live by yourself. No one will even notice that you're gone. Hey, today's my lucky day. While I was waiting for you, I ran into a friend back there by the gate and scored some smack. Life will be great in a little while after I take care of you. No more problems. Ole Tripp will be living the high life soon. You should have minded your own business."

"What do you mean no one will notice that I'm gone?" Delanie yelled. "You don't know anything about me. It's so not going to die with me. You may get me, but you don't have my notes and pictures. You don't know who I've told about all of this."

Tripp paused for a moment, looking puzzled. He hesitated, staring at Delanie with the gun pointed at her. But she noticed his hands trembling.

Tripp stood in the doorway to the stall and stared at her. He was sweating and seemed to pause between each sentence.

Delanie knew he had taken something. She kept her hand on the pitchfork. She would have to do something soon, or he was going to shoot her and leave her in this barn. If she screamed, would anyone hear her?

Tripp paced back in front of the stall. "You have to stop snooping. I'll show you." In an instant, he turned and lunged toward her. She grabbed the pitchfork and rammed it at him with everything she could muster. He had the gun aimed at her head. But in what seemed like slow motion, he let go of the gun, and it flew somewhere behind him when she struck with the metal pitchfork. A blood-curdling scream echoed through the barn, causing the animals to stir and snort. Delanie pierced his right thigh with one of the tines, and blood soaked his jeans and the floor around him. Tripp crumpled in a heap on the hay.

Delanie crawled to her purse, which was closer to him than she wanted it to be. She stood up and stumbled. Holding onto the edge of the stall, flinching in pain as she kicked the gun across the floor. The gun skidded into the stall with the buffalo.

Doubling over, she caught her breath and righted herself. She slid past Tripp and dragged her right leg across the barn. Stopping to catch her breath at the next stall, she could hear Tripp alternating between whimpering and swearing. Propped against the door frame, she rested, trying to calm the jagged breaths and the throbbing in her foot. When her head cleared, she sent a flurry of texts to Steve, John, and Duncan.

When she was dialing 911, two guys in jeans rounded the corner. Delanie shrieked, "That guy in there tried to kill me. He's injured. Go get security. His gun is somewhere over there. I kicked it in the stall with the buffalo. I'm not sure if he has any other weapons."

The taller of the two nodded and took off while the second guy guided Delanie outside of the barn door. "Thanks," she said to him as she continued her conversation with the police dispatcher.

"Yes, I'm sorry. I'm Delanie Fitzgerald, a private investigator. I'm at the Powhatan fairgrounds in one of the barns. This guy tried to kidnap me when I left the bathroom."

"Okay," the female dispatcher said. "I'm alerting state police and the local sheriff. Are you in a safe place?"

"Yes, I'm at the barn door. The guy who grabbed me is injured. He needs an ambulance."

"What is the nature of his injury?" she asked.

"He pulled a gun on me," Delanie said, catching her breath. "He was going to shoot me. I stabbed him in the leg with a pitchfork. He needs attention. He hasn't moved from the stall. There's a lot of blood around him."

"Okay, police and rescue are on their way. Stay put, but make sure that you're safe. How badly are you injured?" the dispatcher asked.

"I can't tell. He stomped on my leg and ankle, but I don't know if it's broken. It really hurts, but I was able to drag it across the barn to the exit. I'm safe, and there's someone else here now. His friend went to find security."

"I'm sorry. I didn't get your name," Delanie said to the young guy leaning on the barn door.

"I'm Dave. My friend Zach went to get security. He should be back in a few minutes."

"Thanks, I'm Delanie. That idiot stuck a gun in my back when I came out of the bathroom and dragged me here. I thought he was going to kill me. He kept babbling and waving the gun around. I think he's on drugs because he said something about buying smack."

Delanie sat in the dirt and gravel with her back to the door. She had to turn to look toward Tripp. He hadn't moved from where he fell on the barn floor, but she could hear his whimpers.

She texted John again to let him know that she was near Barn 12 and that the police were on their way. She was a little miffed that he hadn't responded yet to her first text. After telling her story twice to the sheriff, his deputy, and two state troopers, the EMTs helped Delanie into the back of the ambulance. John had arrived about halfway through Delanie's third rendition of the events.

After quietly listening, he asked, "You okay?" as he moved closer to the back of the ambulance.

"I've felt better," Delanie said. "But I'm glad this is over. Where is he?"

"Over there in that ambulance." He patted her feet, the closest part of her to the open ambulance door. "I'll follow you to the hospital."

"Thanks," she said. "Sorry today didn't turn out like you planned it."

John shrugged as the EMTs closed the ambulance doors. Delanie wasn't sure if they were taking Tripp to the same hospital. She wasn't anxious to see him any time soon. Her last glimpse of him was when they hauled him out of the barn on a gurney. His eyes were closed, and he was the same color as the sheet.

THIRTY-EIGHT

AFTER A THOROUGH check up, John tagged along behind as an orderly pushed her in a wheelchair to the emergency room's main entrance. She felt lucky she'd only ended up with several bruises, a few scratches, and a fractured ankle. Though, she wasn't sure if she would be able to drive any time soon. She was impressed with the hot pink cast and the nifty pair of crutches.

"Wait right here," John said. "I'll go get the truck."

"Okay." She watched him jog through the parking lot. She practiced with the crutches while she waited for John.

While she was leaning on her crutches, Steve pulled up in his cruiser and parked in the fire lane.

"Hey, D," he said. "I thought I'd find you here. Doing okay?"

"Yep. Just a little banged up. And pretty pissed at Tripp. What are you doing here?"

"The task force wants to talk to you again."

"My lucky day," she said. "Does it have to be right now? This hasn't been my best afternoon. And I'm pretty sure that I smell like horse crap."

"No, but the sooner the better. I came by to give you a lift."

"You better be careful. They're going to think that you're my personal chauffeur." She didn't feel like answering any more questions, but if it would help keep Tripp behind bars for a long time, she was in. "Okay," she said with a sigh. "John went to get the truck to take me home. When he gets here, I'll need to tell him about the change of plans."

John pulled up as they were talking, and Delanie hobbled over to the passenger window. Leaving the cruiser running, Steve stepped out and approached the truck.

"John, this is my brother Steve. Steve, this is my date, John Bailey from Amelia County. We were having a nice time at the rodeo before Tripp showed up and decided to pull a gun on me and drag me into a barn." Steve stepped in behind Delanie.

"Hi." John shook Steve's hand through the window. "Pleasure to meet you."

"Nice to meet you, too. Sorry it had to be under these circumstances. The multi-jurisdictional task force wants to talk to Delanie this afternoon. I think she should go downtown."

"Okay," John said, letting out a deep breath. "I can get someone to go with me, and we'll figure out how to get the rental car back to your place. Go with your brother, and I'll bring dinner back to your place."

"I guess this wasn't what you had in mind when you planned our date. Thanks for rolling with the punches. Here's the key." She handed him the plastic fob from the car rental place.

"Somehow you seem to get in the middle of some interesting situations," Steve said, walking toward his car. "Chesterfield's only claims are the property damage that he did to your car and the animal mutilation charge for the possum. The attempted kidnapping and assault happened in Powhatan, but the mayor's murder supersedes all of that."

Delanie waved to John as he drove off, and she followed Steve to his cruiser.

"Is Tripp dead?" she asked, sliding into the front seat. Steve put her crutches in the back.

"No, but he lost a lot of blood. He's probably going to need surgery to repair his thigh. He'll definitely be limping for a while. Who knew you could wield a pitchfork like that? I'm impressed."

"You always said to use what you had in an emergency. Do I need a lawyer?" she asked.

"No. You're the victim in this one. It was clearly self-defense. I called Powhatan on my way over. They found drugs on him, and I'm sure his tox screen won't be clean. He's stacking up charges all over the place."

She hoped Steve was right about her not being a suspect, but she'd keep Chaz's lawyer, Rick Dixon, in her contact list in case the interview didn't go her way.

Steve dropped her at the front doors of the Richmond police building. To Delanie, it felt like she had just been here. A few minutes later, Steve appeared by her side. She followed him through security and upstairs to the same war room where the Richmond detectives had questioned her before.

The audience around the conference table was bigger this time. Detectives Roth and Hagar were talking with two other Richmond PD officers, a woman from the prosecutor's office, and two state troopers.

"Here, sit in this chair. Do you need to prop up your ankle?" Detective Roth asked.

"I'm good. Thanks." Delanie took the seat facing the window that the detective offered. She was surprised at all the concern this time.

Sitting next to her, Detective Hagar introduced the others in the law enforcement contingent.

Detective Roth started the interview, which lasted almost three hours. Delanie was asked to retell the story and videotaped her responses.

"Thank you, Ms. Fitzgerald," Detective Roth said. "We appreciate you helping us with our investigation. I think we have everything we need for now. Someone from the Commonwealth Attorney's office will be contacting you about Kenneth Payne's court appearances and when you'll be needed to testify. We appreciate you coming down here today. I hope you feel better soon."

"Do you have any questions or concerns?" Detective Hagar asked.

"Is there any chance that Tripp could get out on bail?"

"No," Detective Roth said. "We're not finished with all the charges in all jurisdictions, but the list is long. The biggest ones are murder, assault, and kidnapping. He's in the hospital now. When he recovers, he'll be transferred to a lockup where he'll remain until trial. No judge will let him out with that list of charges."

"Good to know," Delanie said. She stood and picked up her purse. The broken strap dragged the ground.

"Thanks again," Detective Roth said. "Please don't hesitate to call us if you have any other questions." He passed more business cards to her from across the table.

She spent the ride from downtown to Chesterfield texting updates to Duncan and Ami. It was a matter of time before the rest of the press would get hold of the capture of the mayor's murderer. Delanie knew that Chaz would be ecstatic with the news. For all his foibles, she was glad that she could prove he didn't kill the mayor. Now, she had to figure out what to do about John Bailey.

THIRTY-NINE

STEVE PULLED HIS cruiser into Delanie's driveway behind John's truck and her rental car. She hobbled up to the front porch and navigated the steps with Steve's help. John followed her to the kitchen with dinner. The possum spot was still visible on the top step even though it had rained last night.

Delanie made her way slowly through the house and managed to get a shower and change into sweats and a T-shirt without assistance. She weighed the danger of leaving Steve alone with John, but she desperately needed a shower. Joining John and Steve in the living room, she plopped down on the couch and propped her leg up on the side. She hoped she hadn't given Steve enough time to tell any embarrassing stories. There was no telling what Mr. Dudley Do Right would tell John about Delanie's past. He lived to embarrass his little sister.

Delanie fidgeted until she got comfortable. Steve said, "I'm going to take off if you're okay. Can I get you a drink or something before I go?"

"I'm fine. It hasn't sunk in yet. Tripp murdered the mayor and tried to kill me. And I guess they're looking into how much the mayor's son was involved."

"Yep," Steve said. "I'm sure that they're looking into

all aspects of Tripp's story. And Chaz Smith should be free soon to continue his antics."

"He's definitely on the slimy side," Delanie said. "But he grows on you after a while. He'll be thrilled with the vindication."

After Steve and John said their goodbyes, John said he brought dinner. "I figured you'd be hungry."

"What'd you bring?"

"Sub sandwiches. Do you want yours heated?" he asked, walking toward the kitchen.

"Yes, thanks."

"What do you want to drink?" he yelled from the kitchen.

"Iced tea is fine. I think there's milk, beer, and maybe OJ in there if tea isn't your thing."

Delanie's phone pinged throughout dinner. She let the calls go to voicemail.

"So, you solved the mayor's murder."

"I guess you and Steve chatted."

John nodded. "I've known what you do for a long time, Delanie."

Delanie's throat tightened. "Time to come clean, I guess. Yes, my partner, Duncan, and I have been working on this for a while. I'm a PI."

"I figured there was more to you than a freelance writer. You didn't try very hard to hide who you were," he said.

She took a deep breath and decided to confront him about his life with The Vibes.

"But you did. Why?" she asked.

"No, not really. I've always been John Bailey. I guess

the good churchgoers would say it was a sin of omission. I never claimed to be anything else."

"Don't you miss the rock and roll lifestyle even a little bit?"

"There's nothing to miss. I have my truck and my farm. I'm happy with my life. I have everything I need." He picked up the sandwich wrappers and cups and took them to the kitchen.

Delanie wanted to ask him about the car wreck to find out who paid off someone to lose the police records. She wanted to keep him talking, but she was afraid that he'd shut down if she brought up his car accident.

"So, no regrets?" she asked when he returned to the living room.

"Nope," he said without hesitation. "I'm who I've always been. That other life died in a reservoir in California." He picked at some imaginary piece of lint on his shirt.

There was awkward silence for a few moments.

"John, I enjoyed our date today even though it didn't turn out as planned. I've enjoyed all of our time together. This was more than business."

John didn't take the bait.

"Do you need me to do anything or get you anything before I take off?"

"No, I'm good," Delanie said. "I appreciate all of your help and patience."

"I've got to feed the animals. They're probably getting cranky right about now."

"I understand," she said, her heart sinking.

"Goodbye," John said, locking the doorknob and pulling the door shut behind him.

Delanie crawled into bed and spent the rest of the evening texting and returning phone messages. She left a voicemail for Rick Dixon in case he and Chaz hadn't heard the news about Tripp's confession. She wasn't sure what she was going to do with John's admission. If he wanted an exclusive relationship, she could wrestle with her conscience and keep his secret. She would feel guilty about it, but she wouldn't reveal it to her client.

Everything with Tripp and John left her in a funk.

Around eight-thirty, she turned off the light. Before she fell asleep, her cell vibrated across the nightstand. "Hello."

"Delanie, how are you? It's me, Chaz. Can you talk? I got a call from Rick about Tripp Payne. I was hoping that I'd catch you."

"How are you?"

"I'm much better now after today's news. I don't know how to thank you. Wow. This is too cool. Rick said that I should be released some time tomorrow. It can't come soon enough for me. Hey, we need to go out to dinner and celebrate the minute I get out. I'll take you out on the town. I promise it will be a night you'll always remember."

"I'm glad to hear that." Delanie wasn't sure if she was ready to celebrate with Chaz. She was satisfied with just his thank you.

"I appreciate all that you've done for me. Call me if I can ever return the favor. You know I'm your biggest fan."

"I'm glad I was able to help," she said.

"My time's almost up. I'll call you when I get settled.

We'll figure out how to celebrate. Thanks again. You're one of the good ones."

"My pleasure," she said. "Take care. I'm happy everything worked out for you." Delanie clicked off the phone and rolled over. She had had enough excitement for one day, and she couldn't muster the energy to think about more face time with Chaz or the fact that a strip club owner was her biggest fan.

FORTY

THE NEXT MORNING, Delanie dragged herself down the stairs and set out for the office. Her phone rang, and she scrambled to pull it out of her purse and balance on the crutches on the gravel driveway.

"Hey, Dunc."

"Hey back. How are you feeling? You had quite the exciting day yesterday. And congrats for getting Tripp to confess."

"I had to stab him in the leg with a pitchfork."

"Whatever it takes. He deserved it."

"Yep. But it ruined my day and probably the rest of the week. I'm still on these stupid crutches. I'm headed in. I want to wrap up a few things," she said.

"You're not taking any time off? You know you can take a day or two off. The world isn't going to end."

"I feel okay. Did we get any good mail? Any news that I should know about?"

"I'm not Emily Jane Mercer's dad," he said.

"Oh, that. You already knew that, huh? Wow. Those results came back a lot sooner than I expected." She rolled her eyes sheepishly, but no one was there to notice.

"It's not funny, Delanie. We'll talk about it when you get in."

"Okay, fair enough," she said, opening the car door. "Anything else I need to know about?"

"Nope. Margaret and I will see you when you get here. Are you okay to drive? I've got plans tonight so I'm going home around three."

"I feel fine. See you in a few." She neglected to mention that the doctor had said to wait until the cast came off before driving. She would be careful. She could drive with her left leg. "Leaving early for an evening of video games?"

"Uh, no. Movies with Evie."

"Evie?"

"I met her at RVACon. She was the one in the Hermione costume and glasses."

"I hope you both have a good time." She smiled. Duncan finally had a date with someone other than Margaret the Wonder Dog.

Delanie easily slid into the front seat of the rental car. Her feet didn't reach the pedals.

Putting her bag and the crutches in front, she had to adjust all the seat settings and the mirrors.

When she turned, she found a plastic jewel box on the seat. Opening The Vibes' CD, she noticed black scribbling on the jacket cover. The CD wasn't hers.

It read: *To Delanie. I hope you enjoy the music and the memories forever. I wish the best for you always. Love, Johnny Velvet. P.S. I'm better as a memory...*

Than as your man. Delanie finished the line in the Kenny Chesney song. She sat in the car for about fifteen minutes, trying to calm the butterflies in her stomach. The excitement changed to curiosity when she realized he must have left this in her car before he came inside her house yesterday.

Not sure what to do next, she turned the CD case over and over in her hands.

Still sitting in the rental car in her driveway, Delanie grabbed her cell and dialed John's number. When she got the "this number is no longer in service" message, she clicked off and redialed. After the second message, she slung the phone onto the passenger seat.

Her stomach dropped to her feet. The butterflies were gone. Her face flushed, and she felt dizzy. She wanted to believe that there was a problem with his cell service, but she knew that the CD sitting next to her was his goodbye. He didn't have the courage to tell her that it was over. He took off again. Just like he did years ago when he abandoned his daughter.

Delanie blinked back the tears and fought the urge to throw up. There was only one way to verify what she already surmised. She had to know for sure.

She drove to his farm in record time. She flew down his driveway, scattering rocks and dust. Coming to a stop behind a large horse trailer, Delanie climbed out, dragging her crutches. She shuffled across the grass past his house to the barn. The only truck in sight was a beige one attached to the trailer with its back door open.

Sticking her head in the open barn door, Delanie yelled, "Hello. Anybody here?"

A small Jack Russell ran to greet her. When she leaned over to pet him, he jumped up and licked her nose. The little dog was exuberant.

A tall man in jeans walked toward her, leading Stewart and Myrtle, the alpacas, and interrupted her. "Can I help you?" he asked. He stopped a few feet in front of her with the animals. The alpacas snorted and stomped their feet.

"I'm Delanie Fitzgerald, a friend of John's. I tried to call him this morning, but I got a message that his cell wasn't in service. I drove out to make sure everything was okay."

"He mentioned you. I'm Charlie. John called me last night and said he had a family emergency. He said he had to go away for a while and take care of some business in Chicago. He didn't know when he'd be back. He asked me to come over and shut up the house and get the animals. Want an alpaca or two?" The tall animals paced as he talked.

"Uh, no. What are you going to do with them?" she asked, still petting the small terrier. Delanie swallowed hard to get rid of the lump in her throat.

"I see you've met Jake the Snake. He hangs with the pack back there. Will, Dave, Eric, and Bob, the Great Dane. I'll take them to my place for now. I have a few acres down the road. I can keep them for a while. If John doesn't come back soon, I'll find someone to take them."

She smiled when she realized John had named the dogs after his Vibes bandmates and manager.

"Did he give you a forwarding address or number?"

"Nope. He was as mysterious as ever. He said he had to go, and he needed my help. It looks like you've made a fast friend there. He seems attached to you. Jake needs a good home."

Scratching the little dog behind the ears, she said, "He's adorable, and I bet he's great company. I don't have the kind of job where I'm home on any kind of regular schedule to take care of him. My heart wants him, but my head is telling me that it wouldn't be fair to any little animal to keep it penned up with my crazy work schedule." After sniffing around her feet, he took off to join the rest of the pack behind the barn. Delanie blinked back tears.

She didn't think her voice would quake, but it did. "And thanks for the information. If you hear from John, tell him I stopped by looking for him. Good luck with all of the animals. I hope he comes back soon."

He nodded and Delanie turned around and headed down the driveway.

She smiled as she put on her sunglasses. The Jack Russell was as cute as he could be, but she couldn't fathom calling him "Jake the Snake." She'd met the original, and they had nothing in common. If he had come home with her, she would have had to rename the dog. Plus, Margaret was the Queen Bee of the office. She wouldn't tolerate the addition of a frisky dog. And that made Delanie wonder how Margaret would get along with Evie.

On her ride back to Chesterfield, Delanie thought about John and chided herself for getting so involved.

She had an overwhelming urge to talk to Duncan. And she had to give Tish Taylor the information that she had paid for and deserved to know. The first thing she'd do back at the office was send John's wineglass to the lab for the overdue DNA testing.

She was proud that Falcon Investigations had found the one and only Johnny Velvet after he had faked his death on that bridge. The pop culture world would be stunned at the revelation, and she was sure that it would be the social media buzz, at least until the next big thing came along.

* * * * *

THESE ARE REAL...

Agecroft Hall—This is a Tudor Home in the Windsor Farms neighborhood. The house was originally built in England. Sold at auction in the 1920s, the new owners shipped and reassembled it in Windsor Farms. The estate and grounds host many special events, including the Richmond Shakespeare Festival.

Amelia Sophia—Amelia County, Virginia, is named for Princess Amelia Sophia, daughter of King George III of England. The county was established from two neighboring counties in 1735. I named my imaginary Bed and Breakfast in honor of the princess.

Bailey/Clay Genealogy—Henry Clay is related to the Baileys, who settled in and around central and western Virginia. I took the liberty of making up the Amelia County family line to fit with this mystery. My mother's Bailey relatives from Roanoke, Virginia, have connections to the Clay family. Thomas Jefferson is also a distant relative of this family line.

Belle Island—This is one of the larger islands in the middle of the James River in downtown Richmond, Virginia. A footbridge under the Lee Bridge provides pedestrian access to the area that once housed a Civil War prison camp, Civil War earthworks, a hydro-electric plant, and a quarry. The island also affords a great view of the capital city and the rapids of the James River.

Brandermill—Awarded the "Best Planned Community in America" in 1977, this was the first community of its kind in Chesterfield, Virginia. Surrounded by the Swift Creek Reservoir, this is a golf course community in the woods.

Byrd Park—Named for William Byrd, this park is located in downtown Richmond. It is home to the WWI Carillion, Dogwood Dell Amphitheater, Swan Lake, Shields Lake, and a tennis complex.

Church Hill—This is an historic neighborhood in Richmond, Virginia, that overlooks the James River. St. John's Church, site of Patrick Henry's "Give me Liberty" speech and Chimborazo Park, the location of the famous Civil War hospital, are key historic sites in the area. Chaz has a townhouse that overlooks the James River in this neighborhood.

Edgar Allan Poe—The famous author, poet, literary critic, and father of the modern mystery lived for a time in Richmond, Virginia. After his parents' deaths, he was taken in by wealthy Richmonder, John Allan. As a young man, he held a literary position at the *Southern Literary Journal*. Poe's mother is buried at St. John's Church (made famous by Patrick Henry's "Give me Liberty" speech). In the summer, the Poe Museum, in the old Stone House, hosts "unhappy hours."

The Fan—This is a neighborhood of about 85 blocks in Richmond. The streets are laid out in a fan shape. It boasts a variety of architectural designs, interesting shops, and unique restaurants. Freeda's is a figment of my imagination.

First Fridays Art Walk—Over forty galleries, shops, and restaurants in downtown Richmond open in celebration of a variety of art, music, and performing arts on the first Friday of each month. Guests can take a walking tour of Richmond's art district.

Kanawha Canal—The Kanawha Canal was built next to the James River in Richmond in the early 1820s. The project was initially supported by George Washington and was designed to connect the James and Kanawha Rivers for transportation of people and goods westward. Parts of the canal have been rebuilt and serve as a focal point for the city. There is a park for walking tours, and visitors can take boat rides.

Kings Dominion—This amusement park, built in Doswell, Virginia, opened in 1975. It was designed similar to its sister park, Kings Island in Ohio. It has a replica of the Eiffel Tower and is famous for its thrill rides and wooden rollercoasters.

Library of Virginia—Like Delanie, this is my favorite library, too, and I'm fortunate to be able to visit often. It is part library, museum, and archives. Hundreds of resources are being digitized monthly and are available online. Their collection is amazing, especially for those doing genealogical research.

Main Street Station—This red-brick train station originally opened in 1901. Located in Shockoe Bottom, it closed in 1975 after Hurricane Agnes flooded most of the downtown area. After serving as a failed mall, nightclub, and state offices, it was refurbished and reopened to rail traffic in 2003. This is my favorite building in downtown Richmond. I made up the restaurant where Delanie met Chaz for a crazy lunch.

Maymont—James and Sallie Dooley deeded Maymont to the City of Richmond. The 100-acre Victorian estate is an example of the Gilded Age's opulence. Visitors can enjoy the specialty gardens, mansion, nature center, and farm in the heart of the capital city.

Richmond Flying Squirrels—This is Richmond's local baseball team. The Squirrels are a farm team for the San Francisco Giants. Their mascot is a large gray squirrel named Nutzy, and their home field is the Diamond on Arthur Ashe Boulevard.

RVA—This is a brand for the Richmond, Virginia, area. Designed by RVA Creates, it's a logo that creates an identity for the capital city and the nearby region.

RVACon—This is a local conference that celebrates comics, popular culture, video gaming, anime, and all things technology. I took the liberty in the story to move the location to the Richmond Convention Center, and I made up the events and contest.

Sears Catalog Homes—While there are several Sears Catalog Homes in Hopewell, Virginia, in the Crescent Hills neighborhood, I took the liberty in this story to move one to Chesterfield County for Delanie's residence. The homes were ordered from the Sears and Roebuck catalog, and they were assembled on your land back in the early 1900s.

Shockoe Slip and Shockoe Bottom—These are neighborhoods in downtown Richmond that lie between the financial district and the James River. A lot of the buildings are restored warehouses, and many of the streets and alleys have cobblestones. Today, the area houses quaint shops and interesting restaurants. A lot of Richmond's nightlife is in this part of town.

Tredegar Iron Works—The Tredegar Iron Works now houses the American Civil War Center. Located next to the James River, visitors can see remnants of the old canal and five buildings where munitions and other iron works were created. It is near the river and the ruins of the canal system. This facility was part of Valentine Museum in the 1990s.

Virginia House—In the 1920s, the Wendell family purchased the original building in England and had it shipped and reassembled on the cliffs of the James River in the Windsor Farm neighborhood.

Virginia Museum of Fine Arts—Built in 1936 as Virginia's art museum, the VMFA is known for its Art Nouveau, Art Deco, and Modern collections. My favorites are the Fabergé eggs, and the Warhol Elvis.

Virginia Rep's Children's Theatre—This is Richmond's children's theatre (formerly Theatre IV). In 2012, the company merged with the Barksdale Theatre to form the Virginia Repertory Theatre. The children's theatre is housed in the former Empire Theatre, built in 1911. It has been renamed the Sara Belle and Neil November Theatre.

Windsor Farms—This is one of the first planned communities in Richmond, Virginia. Development started in 1926. The neighborhood is also home to Agecroft Hall and the Virginia House.

ACKNOWLEDGMENTS

THIS BOOK WOULD not have been possible without all of the wonderful support I received from family and friends.

Many thanks to Stan Weidner for tolerating my writing eccentricities and being supportive of all of the things I get involved with (and drag him into). My parents who instilled in me a lifelong love of reading. Thanks for introducing me to the great world of books. Thanks to Cortney Cain for the early reads and sanity checks. To Meagan and Jocelyn Cain for being my social media gurus, and Bill Cain for keeping us all entertained. And I appreciate all the encouragement from my Bethia UMC family.

I am so grateful for my talented writer friends. Your support is invaluable! Mary Burton and LynDee Walker, I cannot thank you ladies enough for all the great advice!

Thanks to my critique group: Susan Campbell, Sandie Warwick, Cat Brennan, Amy Lilly, K. L. Murphy, Marjorie Bagby, and May Kennedy for all the time you put in to reads and rereads.

Many thanks to Lynda Bishop for her amazing editing skills and Joy Pfister and her wonderful crew at Studio FBJ.

Fiona Jayde does amazing work on the artwork and

covers, and Tina Glasneck makes sure everything is ready to go. I cannot thank you all enough for turning my words into a book.

And I am so grateful for my readers who follow Delanie, Duncan, Margaret, and Chaz's adventures.